'TIS THE SEASON

HATTIE'S STORY

THE MULLED WINE CLUB
BOOK ONE

SUZIE TULLETT

BLOODHOUND
BOOKS

For Betsy and Fred
May our paths cross again

PROLOGUE

SIX MONTHS EARLIER

Huge globules of rain hammered against the shop window and checking my watch, I let out a long sigh. I looked to the heavens. 'Well you can't say I didn't try, Gran.'

Imagining her looking down at me, her short legs dangling over one of the sky's big black clouds, her white wash-and-set, bright blue eyes and kind expression were as clear to me then as they'd always been. She wagged a bony finger my way, as if insisting I gave up far too easily.

'It's all right for you,' I said. 'You're not the one waiting around.'

When I'd decided to form The Knitting Nook's first crochet group, I'd envisaged a room full of fun and laughter. Wool crafters sharing tips and learning new skills. I'd imagined chatter galore as we completed community projects such as post box toppers and baby blankets for the hospital maternity unit. Instead, I was left questioning why, out all the evenings Father Weather could have set the scene for Noah's Ark, he had to choose that one?

I glanced around the peopleless room, disappointed my

efforts had been for nothing. Dragging my feet as I went, I gathered up all the needles and yarn I'd laid out in readiness.

The shop doorbell rang and pausing in my actions, I looked over to see Joyce, a volunteer at the local charity shop *Compassion Corner*, on the threshold. My spirits lifted and telling myself that one attendee was better than none, I again glanced upwards. As usual, Gran was right. I should've had more faith.

Piquing my curiosity, Joyce glanced both up and down the hight street. She came in and shut the door behind her, appearing to breathe a sigh of relief, and she wasn't the only one. My crochet group might well be a success after all! Vindicated, I too could relax.

'Where is everybody?' Joyce took off her sodden rain mac and without even looking for somewhere to put it, handed it straight to me. 'Although I shouldn't be surprised. No one in their right mind would venture out in this downpour.' She reached into her bag and pulled out a towelling face cloth to dry her short grey hair, while I hung her coat on a hook behind the till.

'Maybe everyone's just running late,' I replied. Laying the tools of my trade out for a second time, I indicated that she should take a seat. 'Why don't we give it a few more minutes? You know, in case.'

Joyce smiled as she made herself comfortable. 'Happy to. It's not like I'm in any rush.' She glanced around the shop, as if taking in every detail. 'You've done a great job with this place.'

Appreciating the compliment, I scanned the room. I'd worked hard to bring Gran's wool shop into the twenty-first century and it was good to know I'd done her proud. Every inch had been decorated and modernised. The only thing I'd kept was the shop's name. I'd updated stock and created a seating area for customers to browse patterns at leisure. I'd dotted around knitwear made with my own hands, as examples of what they, too, could achieve. Having extended the range of haberdashery, I'd installed a rail of fabrics to go with numerous small sewing items such as cotton threads, buttons and zips. The whole space had gone from dark and dingy to bright and airy.

Many a Settledown resident had kept an eye on my progress. Calling the fruits of my labour *stunning* and *necessary*, they'd welcomed the changes. But with only Joyce turning up for my crochet group, their praise could have been lip service.

'Have you crocheted before?' I asked.

'Nope.'

'How about knitting?'

'Yes, I've done that.'

I was pleased to hear this: at least Joyce understood yarns.

'But I was rubbish at it,' she added.

The shop door sounded again, and I jumped up from my seat. I didn't recognise the woman entering, but my heart went out to her. Less prepared for the weather than Joyce, she looked like she'd been swimming with her clothes on.

With not even a jacket let alone an umbrella, her wide-leg linen trousers were saturated, and her cotton shirt soaked through. Her clearly expensive sandals were ruined, and I hastened through to the back. 'Here you are,' I said, returning with a towel.

'Look at the state of me.' Accepting my offering, the woman, who appeared to be in her fifties, dried her shoulder-length hair. 'I knew I shouldn't have listened to this morning's weather man.'

Joyce scoffed. 'Don't talk to me about men.'

Ignoring Joyce's quip, I gestured the newcomer forward. 'Glad you could make it.'

She stared at me confused. 'Make what?'

I indicated the workbench. 'Our session.'

Eyeing the tools of my trade, the woman chuckled. 'Do I look like I crochet?'

'I don't know,' I replied in earnest. 'What does a crocheter look like?'

She took in my delicate granny-square cardigan, raising an eyebrow as she turned her attention to the floral blouse and skirt combo that covered Joyce's ample figure. 'Like you two, I suppose. Comfortable.'

'Excuse me,' Joyce said. 'I've never hooked a stitch in my life. I'm only here to save my sanity, because that husband of mine is driving me mad. Talk about under my feet. Every. God damned. Second.' She sighed, wistful. 'I was so looking forward to his retirement. All I can say is, be careful what you wish for.'

In all my preparations for that evening, the one thing I hadn't accounted for was reluctant participants. My gaze went from one to the other.

'If there's anyone who can feel your pain it's me.' The newcomer sat down. 'There's this guy at my office.' She scowled. 'Callum. He's always hovering as well. If you ask me, he's after my job.'

In that moment, if Callum had wanted it, I'd have readily given him mine.

'What is it you do?' Joyce asked.

'Real estate. And unlike Callum who couldn't sell water in a desert, I'm good at it.' The woman glanced around. 'Speaking of deserts, is it me or is it hot in here?' She turned her attention back to Joyce. 'If someone had told me this morning I'd be stumbling into a crochet club, I wouldn't have believed them. I only popped in to get out of the rain.'

With the newcomer apparently staying, I handed each of them a crochet needle and ball of wool.

'I was on my way to visit Mum. You might know her. Maeve Gordon. She lives at the top of the hill.'

Clearly delighted, Joyce threw herself back in her seat. 'Of course, I know Maeve. Lovely woman.'

Ready to commence, I coughed, trying to get their attention.

Joyce cocked her head. 'Don't tell me you're little Erin?'

The newcomer grinned. 'It's a long time since anyone's called me that.'

'I thought you'd gone off to London.'

'Goodness, that was a lifetime ago. I'm over in Leeds now. Have been for years.'

Joyce came over all serious. 'I was sorry to hear about your dad.'

'Ladies, please!' I said.

Shocked into silence, the two of them stared at me.

Erin shifted in her seat. 'I suppose I could give this crochet thing a go while I'm here.' Her eyes lit up. 'I know. Why don't we start with a team-building exercise?' She picked up her yarn. 'Pretend this is a ball and whoever I throw it to has to tell us about themselves.'

Taking it from her, I recoiled at the thought. One of the reasons I loved working for myself was the fact that I didn't have to take part in compliment circles or tangle myself into a human knot. 'Maybe we should learn about each other as we go?'

'You sound like you need a drink,' Erin said.

Considering I felt like I was herding cats, she wasn't wrong.

'I know,' Joyce said. 'Why don't we head over to the pub instead?'

'Great idea,' Erin said. 'And look.' She pointed to the shop window. 'It's even stopped raining.' Wrinkling her nose, she turned to me. 'You have to admit, that sounds a lot more fun than crocheting.'

CHAPTER 1

PRESENT DAY – DECEMBER

'Jingle bells, jingle bells...' Wearing a smile and a red woollen bobble hat, I pulled off my mittens and stuffed them into my duffel coat pockets. 'Jingle all the way...' Singing along to the store's festive soundtrack, I weaved through the Christmas throng, swinging my basket back and forth as I went. 'Oh, what fun it is to ride...' I met the stream of strange looks from fellow shoppers with one grin after another. Anyone would have thought I didn't know I looked a treat and was tone deaf. But one, it was zero degrees outside and wrapping up warm was better than freeze drying. And two, what I lacked in vocal ability I more than made up for in enthusiasm.

I fell silent mid-lyric and coming to an abrupt halt, my eyes widened at a table in front of me. Stacked high with board games, I marvelled at the sight. Monopoly, Cluedo, Trivial Pursuit... all the classics were there. My pulse quickened. If one of those delights didn't ignite Gideon's Christmas spirit, then nothing would.

Stepping towards them, I placed my basket down on the ground and scanned the boxes. Thinking back to Christmases past, childhood festivities wouldn't have been the same without a few tabletop shenanigans. Year after year, Gran and I spent hours creating hotel empires or vying for the ultimate Connect 4 crown – a five-pointed cardboard and tinsel affair I'd made way back when at primary school. I pictured the diadem's tattered and torn state, and wondered how it had continued to survive, and if it would withstand another outing.

I felt a tug on my heart. Gran was the only family I'd ever known, and I'd have swapped that crown for one more Christmas with her any day.

I wondered what Gran would have made of Gideon. Knowing her, she'd have considered him boring. Gran liked big personalities; people who weren't afraid to make a fool of themselves or say what was on their minds. Gideon, on the other hand, was reserved and often kept his thoughts to himself. He was staid and reliable. I sighed. Until recently.

In the aftermath of Gran's passing, Gideon had been my saviour. Up until meeting him, I'd been treading water thanks to funeral arrangements, legalities and what turned out to be Gran's *failing* business. Gideon helped me navigate most of the legal and financial stuff. He'd been my anchor. Thanks to him I'd got to the point where I could think about Gran without bursting into tears of sadness and, if I was honest, frustration. Not that the state of The Knitting Nook accounts should have come as a surprise. Gran was all about enjoying life. For her, the devil was not in the details.

I smiled. Although she could make any occasion fun, Christmas was Gran's speciality. It was a legacy I intended to honour with Gideon that year; despite knowing from experience that he was used to an entirely different way of celebrating.

Gran and I used to pile into the living room in our pyjamas on Christmas morning, eager to rip open our presents in an excited free-for-all. I'd most look forward to the selection box Gran always included in my stocking and while she headed to the kitchen to make bacon sandwiches, I'd demolish a packet of buttons and a Finger of Fudge before the fridge door was even open. Gran might not have been around anymore, but looking into my shopping basket, that hadn't stopped me keeping tradition. There was enough chocolate in there to last me right through to the new year.

Gideon's lot, however, preferred a more structured affair. Only after they'd dressed for and eaten breakfast, did the Mayhews head into the lounge to see if Santa had been. I recalled the previous Christmas, my first without Gran, when Gideon had insisted I'd be better there with him than in Settledown on my own. Each family member took turns to unwrap a single present, while the rest of us were forced to ooh and aah over every single reveal. Of course, people celebrated differently but for a festive hooligan like me, talk about torture. Proceedings took forever.

Almost twelve months on and I'd yet to fully recover. Not only had there been no selection box, I could still feel everyone's eyes on me as I held up my gifted copy of *The Atkins Diet for Beginners.*

'Easier to follow than Keto and Paleo,' Gideon's mum, Serena, said at the time. She clearly thought I was fat, stupid or both.

That might have been my first Christmas with Gideon's family, but I vowed it would be my last.

I shook my mind clear of the unwanted memory and turned my attention back to the mountain of games, wondering which one Gideon might prefer. *Not Twister,* I considered. Too serious for his own good, one look at the spotted mat and he'd declare himself out. *Maybe a compendium would be better?* I pondered. *They've got something for everyone.*

A rhythmic vibration in my pocket interrupted my deliberations and I pulled out my phone. Seeing Gideon's name on the screen, my lips curled into a smile. 'Are you psychic?' I asked upon answering. 'I was just thinking about you.'

'Glad to hear it,' Gideon replied.

'Scrabble or Guess Who?' Sifting through the boxes of board games in front of me, I crossed my fingers hoping for the latter.

'Sorry?'

'Which do you prefer?'

'I don't know. I've never thought about it, why?'

'Because it's what people do at this time of year. Play board games.'

Gideon sighed. 'Please tell me you're not out spending again, Hattie. We've talked about this.'

Being in a relationship with an accountant might have had its perks. Like being introduced to the 50-30-20 money management rule. But when it came to certain times of year it also had its downsides. Like being introduced to the 50-30-20 money management rule.

Despite Gideon's resistance, I was determined to create the best Christmas ever and I pictured the two of us enjoying a cosy Yuletide evening in front of a roaring fire. We each held a glass of mulled wine in one hand and we were passing a dice shaker between us. 'Now's not the time to play Ebeneezer Scrooge. I'm being serious here.'

'So am I. Anyway, never mind that. I'm calling about tonight.'

Closing my eyes for a second, I let the box in my hand drop. I knew what was coming. Gideon was yet again about to tell me he had a target still to meet and that with the holidays around the corner, his employer was breathing down his neck. 'Please don't say it.'

'But I–'

'Promised?'

I considered the number of times Gideon had reneged on our plans at the last minute of late. He'd missed Settledown's

Halloween and bonfire night celebrations; gone AWOL for Erin's big birthday bash; and I'd still not forgiven him for passing on the local cinema's digitally remastered screening of *It's a Wonderful Life*. Only my favourite festive movie ever: that disappointment stung the most.

A screening at Settledown Picture House was like stepping back in time. Built in the early 1900s, it had one auditorium, home to rows of faded burgundy seats with wooden armrests. Intermissions were still a thing and halfway through every film, huge red curtains swished in front of the screen as the lights came on and an usherette appeared in the aisle to sell ice creams. It was the perfect setting in which to watch George Bailey's story unfold.

Waiting in the foyer, holding two large cartons of popcorn, I knew Gideon would love all the nostalgia as much as I did, and I struggled to contain my excitement. But as the minutes ticked by and showtime neared, it was harder to ignore the growing chink in my enthusiasm. My gaze went from the building entrance to that of the auditorium, and wondering where Gideon could have got to, I refused to believe he wasn't coming. Giving him every excuse going, I told myself he was stuck in traffic, he couldn't find a parking space, even that he'd got lost... The box office attendant had obviously seen it all before. By the time I accepted defeat, his expression oozed pity.

About to repeat his apologies, Gideon might insist he didn't have any choice when it came to his work commitments, but I had to question whether sometimes they were a convenient excuse.

'I did promise, yes,' Gideon replied. 'And I'm sorry.'

Standing there, I wasn't sure who I was more disappointed in. Me, for believing Gideon wouldn't let me down again. Or him for daring to after giving his word.

'You know what it's like around here. The bosses are

constantly on my case. I'm dealing with a stream of tax deadlines and year-end reports, and I've still got new accountancy laws and regulations to get my head around.'

I rolled my eyes. He was like a stuck record. 'I understand all that, but you're not the only one with a lot on.'

A fellow customer appeared to check out the game table and I found myself distracted. Taller than anyone I knew, he looked down at me with deep brown eyes that were warm and friendly. He had a square jaw and a dimpled chin, and his smile revealed the most perfect of teeth. He reminded me of a younger Keanu Reeves. Embarrassed to be arguing in front of him, I lowered my voice and turned away. 'December's the shop's busiest time of year too, Gideon, but you know what? I still put us first.'

'So why aren't you there?'

'Where?'

'At the shop?'

As I realised what he was referring to, a flush crept across my cheeks. 'You know why.'

'Do I?'

I looked down at my feet, not wanting to answer his question out loud. 'Because Wednesday is half-day closing,' I finally said.

'So you're a part timer. I rest my case.'

Opting for Twister, Keanu mouthed an apology as he reached in front of me to get it. He gave me a nod and another smile as he went on his way.

I almost swooned as I watched the once seen never forgotten chap disappear into the crowd.

'Hattie, are you still there?'

I forced myself back to the matter at hand. 'That's not the case and you know it. It's not my fault Settledown's old school.'

Gideon laughed. 'Even so, you can hardly compare your job to mine. Sitting behind a till isn't exactly brain work.'

I rolled my eyes. Because tapping numbers into a cash

register is so much easier than tapping them into a calculator... I wondered what had happened to the Gideon I'd first met. Back then he'd said turning Gran's little wool shop from a beloved but neglected concern into a thriving enterprise was something I should be proud of. He'd admired my business acumen and creative thinking.

'Besides, it's not like we *never* have time together,' Gideon said. 'Plus we have the holidays to look forward to. Come January, we'll be so sick of each other we'll be glad to get back to work.'

'That's not the point.' I chewed on the inside of my cheek. For a man of few words, he seemed to have a lot to say. 'Gideon, there's only so many times a woman can come second to–'

'I know. But Julia and I–'

'Julia? I was going to say *second to a spreadsheet*.'

'Come on, Hattie. She's a work colleague.'

'A colleague that can moonlight as a Priyanka Chopra lookalike.' I looked down at the thick green tights and blue wellington boots that poked out from under my duffel coat. Attire that Julia/Priyanka wouldn't be seen dead in. I suddenly felt like a bad Paddington Bear knock-off. 'You do know she can take people out with her eyelashes,' I said. 'A simple coordinated blink and flick of her head, and that's it. You're done for. Rumour has it she's a paid assassin.'

'Tell you what, why don't I swing by when I'm done?'

'So now I'm meant to sit around waiting for you, am I? Like I don't have anything better to get on with.'

'Well, do you?'

Frustrated, I tipped my head back and looked skyward. Considering I'd already set the evening aside for us, we both knew the answer to that. I swapped my phone from one hand to the other. 'What time are you thinking?'

'I'm not sure.'

Letting Gideon's words hang in the air, my irritation grew. He seemed to be making the transition from *attentive boyfriend* to *can't be arsed* a bit too seamlessly for my liking. Fed up with coming second place to his job, I wanted to tell him not to bother, but opening my mouth to speak, I wavered. 'Look it's fine,' I said instead. Even if he did call round, I supposed I'd only end up equally annoyed when he fell asleep on the sofa. 'We can rearrange. Just get done what you need to get done.'

'And you're definitely okay with that?' Gideon asked.

I wasn't at all, but what choice did I have? 'I am.'

Gideon perked up. 'Honestly, Hattie, this time I really will make it up to you.' Whether he meant that or not, at least he had the decency to sound like he did.

I heard Julia's voice in the background. 'Time to go, Gideon,' she said.

'Sorry, Hattie. These tax calculations aren't going to solve themselves. I'll give you a call tomorrow, yeah?'

'When tomorrow?' I asked as the line went dead.

CHAPTER 2

*P*utting on my coat and donning my woolly hat, I steeled myself to head downstairs and out into the cold night air. Still in the throes of self-indulgence thanks to Gideon's no-show the previous night, I resisted the temptation to take them off again in favour of staying home. If anyone could pull me out of my pity party, it was Erin and Joyce. Our crochet club might exist in name only as a ruse to give Joyce some much-needed me-time, but in reality, we all benefited.

Over the last six months the three of us had built up a solid friendship, even though on paper you couldn't get a trio of more different women. Erin, the hard-nosed businesswoman who knew what she wanted and went for it; Joyce, a retiree who'd been married forever and looked like she belonged to the Jerusalem and jam brigade; and then there was me. I sighed. A thirty-one-year-old simp who had everything I could want except a devoted boyfriend.

Making my way downstairs, I let myself out of the shop, locking the door behind me. The pavement glistened with frost; icy sparkles that shimmered in tandem with Settledown's twinkling Christmas lights. Heading down the road towards the town square with its humongous brightly lit Norway Spruce, I took in the festive window displays.

That year's theme was Hoffman's *The Nutcracker and The Mouse King*, and traders including me had been keen to embrace it. As well as the title characters, exhibits included clockwork castles, Princess Pirlipats and doll kingdoms. There were Christmas trees adorned with walnuts for baubles, and little mice peeking from behind perfectly wrapped gift boxes. Warm accent lighting and rich backgrounds of red, green and gold made each scene come alive. While Settledown was picture postcard pretty no matter the time of year, at Christmas, it was magical.

The Royal Oak came into view and hastening towards its entrance, I pushed open its heavy wooden and glass-framed door. The warmth emanating from the open fire with its huge stone tinsel-covered mantel felt welcoming. But as much as I'd have preferred a more convivial seat next to the flames, thanks to Erin's fluctuating body temperature, I knew we had to sit as far away from the heat as possible.

Taking off my hat and unbuttoning my coat, I scanned the room, wondering if the place had been worth opening. A young couple, deep in conversation, sipped on mugs of mulled wine at one table, while an older pair with their dog, took up another. Ted, the pub's most loyal of clientele, sat pint in hand, in his usual spot propping up the bar. As for other customers, there weren't any. Not that I should have been surprised to find the place quiet. Settledown might be busy come weekend when the tourists landed, but for most of the locals, winter had always been a time of hibernation.

I cocked my head in confusion. Not the most chatty of bartenders, Danny would seat himself at the far end of the bar, scrolling through his phone in the hope no one could spot him. That evening he was nowhere to be seen. Instead, a new guy had taken up residence. I couldn't see his face as he was head down, concentrating on a sketch he drew.

I coughed loudly to get his attention, and he immediately dropped his pencil and looked up. I smiled. 'It's you,' I said of the once seen never forgotten chap.

He gave me a cheeky wink. 'It was the last time I looked.'

A sense of humour and good looking. I was impressed. 'You don't remember me, do you?'

His face broke into a grin. 'How can I forget? Navy duffel, green tights, blue wellies?'

I blushed. No wonder he recognised me. Said out loud, my outfit sounded quite the combination, and I could think of better ways to make an impression.

'What can I get you?' he asked.

'Hattie!' a woman called out.

I spun round to see Joyce, sat at a table tucked in the corner by the Christmas tree. I chuckled, realising it was no wonder I hadn't noticed her. Rammed with crimson baubles and gold trimmings, the tree branches were the perfect camouflage for Joyce in her red and green sweater. 'It's okay,' I said to the new barman. 'I'm good thanks.'

When it came to our Crochet Club, it was customary for the first to arrive to get the drinks in and as I made my way over, I was ready for the vin blanc that Joyce had waiting. 'Boy do I need this,' I said. Sitting in the seat opposite her, I picked up my glass. 'I'm having one of those weeks.'

'Good to know it's not just me.'

'I take it Erin's running late?'

Joyce shrugged. 'It looks that way.'

I observed my friend's demeanour. Usually a woman with

presence, she sat hunched and spiritless. 'Is everything okay?' I asked.

'Not really. But I'll live.' She picked at the corners of a beermat. 'I read a news article this morning saying the divorce rate amongst the over sixties is rising.' She looked at me direct. 'I, for one, can appreciate why.'

My heart went out to her. When it came to his pensioner status, her husband had still yet to adjust, turning Joyce's twilight years dream into a never-ending nightmare. 'I take it things are no better?'

'Nope. If anything, they're getting worse.' She went from picking at to tearing the beermat. 'It's not that I don't understand. Of course, I do. Going from working all hours to not working at all is bound to have an impact. But he doesn't even try to enjoy his newfound freedom.' She scoffed. 'Although it's hardly *new*, is it? He retired months ago.' She gathered the shredded cardboard into a neat pile. 'It's like living with some rescued street dog that can't quite settle.' She drank a mouthful of wine. 'It'd be kinder to have him put down.'

I was used to Joyce talking about her marital woes, but that was blunt even for her and I let out a nervous chuckle. 'I have the opposite problem. You'd be lucky to find me and Gideon in the same room.'

'Now you're just rubbing it in.'

I gave Joyce a sympathetic smile.

'I got fired today,' she said.

I cocked my head. 'From the charity shop? They can't do that.' While volunteers came and went over the years, Joyce was Compassion Corner's single die-hard. She'd been there so long she was seen as part of the fixtures and fittings.

'They can and they have.'

'But why?'

'Because not content with dropping in to annoy me time and

time again, Richard decided to give pro bono advice on how to better run the place.'

'Oh, Joyce, he didn't.'

'Oh it doesn't end there. Fed up with his advice being ignored, this afternoon he took it upon himself to put his words of wisdom into practice. You know, change things around a bit.' She rolled her eyes. 'Although when I say "a bit", he caused complete chaos. The whole shop was a mess. It's no wonder the manager reached boiling point.'

I pictured the scene. Finding it funny-not-funny, I put a hand up to my mouth to hide any hint of amusement.

'I don't blame her. What choice did she have? Letting me go was the only way she could get rid of *him*.' Joyce drank yet more wine. 'I keep thinking I should pack him off to Nial's.'

My eyes widened. 'In Australia?'

'Well if he won't listen to me, he might listen to his son and I know for a fact time apart would do us good.'

'But sending him all that way... Isn't that a bit extreme?'

'I know Olivia wouldn't mind, and the kids would love to see their granddad.' Joyce let out a dry laugh. 'Of course, I'd have to drug him first. Getting Richard on a plane of his own free will is nigh on impossible. Why do you think we holiday in Cornwall?'

'*You* could go? Give yourself a break.'

'And leave Richard on his own? You really think he'd cope?' Joyce chuckled. 'The man would wither away and die.'

I reached over and squeezed her hand. 'Things will get better.'

Joyce took a deep breath and exhaled. 'Thank you.'

'What for?' I asked.

'For being here. Without Compassion Corner, this club of ours will be the only thing keeping me sane.'

I smiled. It had been clear from our first meeting back in the summer that Erin and Joyce had no interest in wool crafts.

Glasses of vino and a good natter were more their thing and admittedly, I loved them for it. 'That place can't operate without you. They'll be begging you to come back before you know it.'

'Even so, I don't know what I'd do without you and Erin.'

Catching sight of the pub door opening, I looked over to see Erin make her entrance. 'Speak of the devil,' I said.

CHAPTER 3

Bounding through the pub door, Erin put a hand up to acknowledge us and made her way over. 'Apologies for the tardiness, ladies. There are some big changes taking place at the office and I ended up staying later than planned.' She took off her coat and hung it on the back of her chair. 'Still, I'm here now.' She sat down and picked up her drink. 'Cheers, everyone.'

Thinking Erin could teach my boyfriend a thing or two, I scoffed. 'I wish Gideon understood the concept of better late than never.'

Joyce sighed. 'I wish Richard was still doing overtime.'

With her glass already at her lips, Erin lowered it again. 'I can see tonight's going to be fun.'

'Don't mind me.' Joyce downed the last of her wine. 'My problems are nothing a divorce lawyer can't sort.'

Erin laughed. 'And you wonder why I choose to stay single.'

'In my case, I may as well be on my own. Gideon's not exactly attentive these days.'

'If you're both trying to make me jealous,' Joyce said. 'It's working.'

Erin shook her head. 'You know what Richard needs?' She took off her cardigan and pushed up her shirt sleeves.

'A job,' Joyce replied.

'A sense of responsibility. Get him doing something around the house. A bit of DIY, garden landscaping, anything that gets his brain working and his hands moving. That's what I plan to do when I retire.'

I nearly choked on my drink. 'Like that's ever gonna happen.' In the six months I'd known Erin, if there was one thing I'd learned, it was that she lived to work, not worked to live. 'They'll have to drag you out of that office kicking and screaming.'

Erin looked at me direct. 'Which is what's going to happen if Callum has his way. That weasel's made it clear to anyone who'll listen he thinks I'm losing my edge.' Reminiscent of a James Bond baddie, she narrowed her eyes and formed a steeple with her hands. 'But don't worry I'm one step ahead.' Erin picked up her drink again. 'At the moment, I'm more worried about Mum. Did I tell you her new neighbours have moved in?'

'No.' Always one for a bit of gossip, Joyce perked up.

'I don't know much about them yet, but from what Mum says, they're a father and son duo.'

'No mother on the scene.' Joyce leaned forward. 'Interesting.'

'Why would that worry you?' I asked.

'I suppose I don't want them taking advantage. The son is especially getting pally, and *you* know what Mum's like, Joyce.'

Joyce nodded. 'Oh, I do.'

'She'll help anyone.'

'Oh, she would,' Joyce said.

'Not that there's anything wrong with that,' Erin said. 'But she's getting on a bit now and as much as I hate to say it, she's not the woman she once was.' She took a deep breath and exhaled. 'As for you, Hattie...'

Erin had never been one to properly share and I wasn't surprised at her sudden change of conversation.

'Your issue is nothing some beautiful lingerie and come-to-bed eyes won't solve.'

Having never understood the concept of bedroom dress-up, I squirmed at the thought.

'Unless he's getting it from somewhere else?' Erin pondered. 'Because, trust me, if he is, there isn't a pair of knickers on the planet that would sort that mess out.'

Again, I nearly choked on my wine. 'Believe me, Gideon is not that kind of man.' I pictured him in one of the many V-neck sweaters he owned, absorbed in the latest version of some accountancy manual that rested on his crossed-legged knee. 'You do know a good day out for him is a trip to an abacus museum. No way would he have an affair.'

Erin smiled. 'In that case, you've nothing to worry about and I've got the perfect plan.'

'Plan?' I didn't like the sound of that.

'I might not be in a relationship, Hattie, but that doesn't make me a numpty when it comes to men. I do have some experience. Believe me, Gideon will forget all about work. He'll only have time for you once I'm done.'

'I wish Richard would have an affair,' Joyce said. 'Not that it's ever going to happen. How can it? Glued to me almost twenty-four seven, he'll never get the opportunity.'

'Speaking of romance...' Erin nodded to the bar. 'Who's the new guy?'

As if in an episode of *The Golden Girls* meets *Sex in The City*, we all stared at the man, letting out a collective dreamy sigh.

'His name's Alex,' Joyce replied. 'Apparently, the brewery has had a restructure and Danny's been moved on. They've got big ideas for this place, and insist Alex is the man for job. They want to attract a more modern clientele. There's talk of a big refurbishment in the new year.'

'I'm not sure the locals will approve,' I said.

'From where I'm sitting, things look better already,' Erin said.

'He was poached from some fancy cocktail bar,' Joyce continued. 'A French sounding place.'

My eyes lit up. 'Le Bonsoir, I'm betting. Gideon took me once. The mixologists there are brilliant, and their creations divine.' I giggled. 'Not to mention potent.' I recalled how Gideon had had to pour me into a taxi to get us back to mine and then slide me out once we landed. Guiding me through the shop, he got fed up with trying to coax a wittering and giggling me upstairs. In the end he simply threw me over his shoulder and carried me in a fireman's lift. 'Their raspberry martini cocktail is to die for.' As I drank a sip of wine, my smiled faded. Less appealing were Gideon's complaints after pulling a muscle in his back.

'We should go one evening,' Erin said. 'Make a proper night of it.'

'I must warn you it's pricey. Hence, our one and only visit. Gideon never suggested it again.'

'Maybe Alex could get us a discount? You know, organise mate's rates,' Joyce said. 'According to him, he worked there for years.'

'Must have been his night off when I went,' I said. Not that I recalled much about that evening anyway.

'What is he doing?' Erin asked. 'He hasn't put that pencil down since I got here.'

'Sketching. He's a budding artist,' Joyce replied. 'He showed me a couple of his drawings and I have to say, he's pretty good.'

I couldn't believe all the information she'd gleaned. Joyce and I both lived in the same town, knew the same people and frequented the same places, but while I might have a broad understanding of other's lives, she seemed to hold dossiers on everyone's past, present and hopes for their future.

'His family live further up north.' Joyce nudged my arm and dipped her chin. 'Near Gideon's hometown, in fact.'

'And you know all this how?'

'How do you think?' She looked at me like I was stupid. 'I asked him.'

As if sensing he was being talked about, Alex looked up from his drawing. He smiled, causing the three of us to swoon.

'He's staying here in the pub for now, but after Christmas he's hoping he can find a new place to live,' Joyce said.

'I can't imagine that'll be easy,' Erin said, putting her real estate head on. 'Not around here. Rentals hardly ever become available and when they do, they're snapped up in hours.'

Joyce's gaze fast went from Alex to me. 'You have a spare room, Hattie. Perhaps he could rent that?'

'Excuse me?' I couldn't believe she'd suggest such a thing.

'Well it's sitting there empty.'

I laughed. 'I don't think so.'

'Why not?'

I wanted to say because he was a stranger. I knew nothing about him. But thanks to Joyce's information dump the latter wasn't strictly true. 'Because I like my own space.'

'But the money he'd pay in rent could offset some of the costs from modernising the shop,' she said. 'Surely, it's worth thinking about?'

I rolled my eyes. 'You're beginning to sound like Gideon.'

Erin twirled her hair around her index finger. 'A bit of extra cash. A nice view at the breakfast table...' She sighed. 'I'd call that a win-win.'

'Then you take him in,' I said. 'I have enough problems with *one* man in my life. Why would I want *two*?'

CHAPTER 4

The last place I'd expected to find myself on the first late-night shopping event of the season, was in an expensive lingerie-come-sex shop. I usually spent it picking up sweets and knick-knacks to fill Christmas stockings, not buying flimsy date night accoutrements.

Upon our arrival, Joyce had chuckled at my reluctance and called me Miss Priss, but I was happy in my prudishness. Stood in the queue to the till, all I wanted to do was get out of there. Trying to swallow my embarrassment, I questioned why I'd let my friends talk me inside, never mind into buying something.

I heard unnecessary tutting and grumbling from behind me. Everyone knew December was retail's busiest time of the year.

'What's the hold-up?'

Everyone except the woman further back in line, it seemed, who unlike me, didn't care who clocked her presence. Busy with it, staff were obviously doing their best to keep rails and shelves well stocked. I raised an eyebrow. Until that evening, I'd never heard of a boneshaking wand or handheld curvy. Or fully appreciated that ignorance was, indeed, bliss.

My gaze fell on my two friends and observing them

manhandle the more specialised wares on offer, I cringed at their lack of shame.

Wearing a sexy Santa hat and a feather boa, Joyce stuck out her backside, waiting for an eye-masked Erin, paddle at the ready, to spank her. The two of them snorted with laughter, adding sound to the indelible image that would be forever imprinted on my brain.

Shaking my head, I turned away, but couldn't resist another quick glance. Erin and Joyce had moved on to the dildo section and I wished the place sold invisibility cloaks.

'Someone's in for a treat,' the shop assistant said when I, at last, reached the front of the line.

My blushes deepened. According to Erin, the scarf style plunge bra didn't just enhance a woman's cleavage, its lacy fabric was guaranteed to seduce. And of course, in her opinion, I just had to buy the matching knickers.

When it came to underwear, I'd yet to sample the full bellied cosiness of the high brief, but I still went for comfort over aesthetics, a quality you could find in the women's department of a supermarket. What you couldn't find in places like Asda, however, were the edible licks and massage oils Erin also recommended. 'If we can't spoil loved ones at Christmas, when can we?' Panic hit me. Far too much information to give to a stranger, I couldn't believe I'd just said that. 'I mean ourselves... If we can't spoil ourselves.'

As the shop assistant rang up my items up, I watched the total amount increase at an exponential rate. Dreading the cost, my heart dropped to the pit of my stomach.

The assistant nodded to the payment machine, and I delved in my bag for my purse. I crossed my fingers on one hand, while holding my debit card over the screen using the other. The subsequent bleep sounded more like a yelp, causing me to tense on the payment machine's behalf. While having my card declined would be bad enough, to have it declined in a shop that sold sex toys would be downright humiliating.

Waiting for the words *payment accepted* to flash up, I pretended not to notice the seconds go by.

'What's taking so long?' the woman behind me asked.

I pretended not to notice that too.

At last, the screen changed in my favour, and I could breathe again.

The shop assistant smiled. 'Would you like a receipt?'

I fast shook my head as I tucked away my purse. 'No thank you.' It was one thing knowing what I'd just spent, having the physical evidence to prove it was something else. 'When you're ready, ladies,' I said to Erin and Joyce, desperate to get out into the fresh sexless air. 'I'll be outside.'

As I stepped out into the street, an icy wind whipped around my face, perfect for cooling my cheeks down. My feet burned, having walked for what felt like miles, and the handles of all the bags I carried dug into my palms.

I looked up to the sky. Even in the darkness, it appeared heavy and foreboding. However, with no snow forecast, the looming dark clouds indicated yet more rain; weather that made me want to head home, light the fire and snuggle down for what was left of the evening.

'Spotted anything exciting up there?' a male voice asked.

I immediately recognised it as belonging to Alex and smiling, I lowered my gaze to meet his. Grinning back at me, he had a cheeky glint in his eyes and his cheeks were pink from the cold. 'Shouldn't you be working?' I asked, surprised to see him.

'It's my night off, which I'm using to start my Christmas shopping. Not that I'm achieving much.' He indicated his bags. 'So far, I've picked up four selection boxes and a *Guinness World Records*.'

Considering what I'd just bought, the last thing I wanted was

Alex comparing purchases and I manoeuvred my most recent out of sight.

'Before you ask, no, they're not connected,' Alex continued. 'There are no plans to eat chocolate against the clock and my name will not feature in a future edition.'

I let out a laugh. 'Spoil sport.'

'I have a nephew who loves random facts and figures. For example, did you know the record for most selfies taken in three minutes is 184?'

'I did not.'

'Neither did I until I picked up this little beauty.' Again, he indicated his shopping. 'I can't wait to see that boy's face on Christmas morning. He's gonna love it.'

Alex's nephew wasn't the only one by the sounds of it.

'Anyway, time to get back to it,' Alex said. 'These presents aren't going to buy themselves.'

His festive enthusiasm was infectious, and I forgot all about my aching feet. 'Okay. Well nice to have seen you.'

Setting off down the street, Alex turned to face me as he went. Walking backwards, he gave me the most gorgeous of smiles. 'Merry Christmas!' he called out.

I shook my head and chuckled, my smile continuing even after he faced forward again. Watching him disappear into the crowd, I considered how much fun Alex seemed. And positive. Characteristics that reminded me of Gran.

The shop door slid open behind me, and my laughter-filled friends appeared.

'Shall we try out that mulled wine cart we spotted earlier?' Joyce asked.

Erin grinned. 'I'm up for that.'

I opened my mouth to explain I was ready for home but before I could answer, Erin had linked arms with both me and Joyce, and we were on our way.

The cart's line of customers was longer than I'd hoped and unable to face another queue, I spotted a vacant table. 'Shall I snag that before someone else does?'

'Go ahead,' Erin replied. 'We'll get the drinks.'

Heading over, I placed my bags down and took a seat. Glad to be off my aching feet at last, I breathed a sigh of relief. I savoured the aroma of oranges, cloves, cinnamon and red wine that floated on the air. The cart vendor, wearing a hoodie under his padded jacket to stave off the cold, sang along to the Christmas carols being piped through the city centre's speaker system. As I watched him, I shivered in the cold, my body shaking in harmony with the music.

A little boy giggled as he ran by, quickly followed by a man whom, going off his likeness and exasperated expression, I assumed to be the boy's father. They headed towards the square's nativity scene, where a gathering oohed and aahed over baby Jesus. I observed couples holding hands, some snuggling close as they admired shop windows, while teenagers congregated in groups. Women flitted from one store to another as if determined to get a head start on their gift shopping. All against a backdrop of Christmas lights and festive displays.

Erin and Joyce pulled me out of my reverie when they finally landed, bringing with them three lots of mulled wine and a plate of mince pies.

While they got themselves comfortable, I reached for a hot mug, and wrapping my hands around it, took a sip. 'Perfect,' I said, as the soothing liquid warmed my insides.

'Don't get too comfortable,' Erin said. 'We might not be finished yet.' She delved into her handbag and pulling out a to-do list, began to read. 'Tell me, when's your Christmas tree coming?'

'Tomorrow,' I replied.

Erin mumbled to herself, as if placing a mental tick next to each item she noted. She looked from the list to Joyce and me with a satisfied smile. 'Our work is done.' Erin lifted her mug for us all to celebrate with a ceramic clink. 'Cheers, ladies. We have achieved our objectives.'

'I'm still not convinced all this is necessary,' I said, gesturing to the shopping bags at my feet. 'It feels a bit manipulative, like I'm toying with Gideon. As if our relationship's some sort of game.'

'Get used to it,' Joyce said. 'In my experience, it's a case of needs must.'

'Mine too.' Erin scowled. 'Unfortunately.'

'Take tonight,' Joyce said. 'As far as Richard's concerned, we're both round at yours learning how to Jacob's ladder.'

The fact Joyce had even heard of that crochet stitch was impressive.

'Am I lying to my husband?' Joyce asked. 'Definitely. But do I have good reason? Yes, I do.'

I narrowed my eyes, unconvinced.

'Look at it this way,' Joyce carried on. 'That one white lie isn't just saving my sanity; it's keeping me out of either the divorce court or prison. And for that alone, it's worth it.' She bit into a mince pie. 'Richard benefits in that he gets to keep his life and his wife. And I get time to myself.' She shrugged, evidently guilt free. 'It's a win-win for both of us.'

'But aren't you worried he'll find out?' I asked. 'And feel betrayed?'

'Who's going to tell him?'

'He must've noticed you're not actually doing any crocheting?'

'One step ahead of you,' Joyce said. 'You know that cardigan you had on display that I just couldn't live without? And the lovely green cushion cover with the raspberry flower design?'

My eyes widened. 'You didn't tell him you made them?'

'I did.' Joyce grinned. 'And I don't feel bad about that either.'

I had to admire her ingenuity.

'Remember, most people lie to their spouses because they're playing away. I'm the opposite. I'm doing it to keep us together. I could never do to Richard what Gloria Chalmers's husband did to her.' She pondered a moment. 'Thinking about it, you could learn a lot from that woman, Hattie.'

'Like what?' The only thing I knew about Gloria was that she taught at Settledown primary school, and I liked to think I was more intellectually advanced than that.

Joyce took a sip of mulled wine and got herself comfortable. 'Just like Gideon, her husband suddenly started working extra-long hours. And like you, Gloria thought nothing of it.'

'I think we know where this is going,' Erin said.

'But then her husband got secretive,' Joyce carried on. 'Possessive of his mobile phone, sneaking off into another room when it rang, you get the gist. After that, he started picking fights over the simplest of things.'

'Textbook,' Erin replied. 'I bet he smartened himself up as well.'

Joyce let out a dry laugh. 'Only when he went out, because heaven forbid he put effort in for his wife.'

Looking like she'd stepped in something horrible, Erin pursed her lips.

'Then weird things started to happen,' Joyce continued. 'His taste in music changed, stuff like that. Gloria hadn't heard of half the bands he was listening to. She had her suspicions, naturally. But whenever she raised them, he told her she was imagining things and tried to make her feel bad for thinking that way.'

My heart went out to Gloria. 'So what happened in the end?'

'Six months later he left her for his secretary.' Joyce threw her hands in the air. 'Turns out Gloria was right all along.'

My gaze flitted from Joyce to Erin and back again. Taking in their knowing expressions, I couldn't believe they thought I was in the same position. 'But apart from working late, Gideon isn't doing any of that.'

'And he might never,' Joyce said. 'But at least thanks to women like Gloria you know what signs to look out for.' She folded her arms across her chest.

'And if my plan doesn't work,' Erin said, indicating my shopping bags. 'I suggest you open your eyes.'

'And there you have it. The perfect chignon in five easy steps.' The YouTube vlogger tilted her head, offering me and the rest of her online audience an equally perfect smile.

I wasn't impressed. With her brilliant white teeth and flawless make-up, she could have given herself a buzz cut, and she'd have still looked good.

The vlogger panned her camera around to show off her sophisticated updo. Combining sexy bedhead with a polished French twist, she'd done what she'd set out to do and produced a style that worked from *everyday hair through to special occasion*.

I sighed, knowing it didn't take a genius to see that I had not.

I picked up a hand mirror and held it at the back of my head. Using it to assess my efforts in the dressing table, I didn't know whether to laugh or cry. Instead of creating a classically loose knot, my chignon lacked the intended carefree volume; it resembled a giant inedible bun. Rather than the two or three bobby pins I was supposed to need, my updo had its own scaffolding tower, and as far as romantic wisps were concerned, after half a can of hairspray they were just wishful thinking. Mimicking the vlogger, I, too, angled my head to one side. 'Five easy steps, I don't think so.' She clearly hadn't accounted for the *wash and leave* crew. People like me who had a favourite hair bobble.

Telling myself I'd never make a hairdresser and should stick to selling wool, I swiped the vlogger's face off the screen and shut down the app completely. I pulled my fancy knickers out from between my bum cheeks, with no choice but to hope they and the matching plunge bra worked their magic and kept Gideon's gaze from straying too far upwards.

I stuffed my phone into my dressing gown pocket and leaving the mirror behind, made my way downstairs trusting I'd done a better job of dinner.

Pausing in the lounge, I breathed in the woody scent of the humongous Douglas fir that filled the window. I couldn't count the number of times I'd been tempted to cover its branches in a mass of baubles and tinsel, but giggling at thoughts of the evening ahead, I told myself the delay was worth it. Gideon and I were about to enjoy our first date since he reneged and like Erin said, what could be more romantic than chatting over an intimate meal, putting on some Christmas tunes and decorating a Christmas tree? Romance was definitely in the air.

In the kitchen, I smiled at the laid table. The vintage holly-patterned crockery set I'd inherited from Gran sat in readiness on a crisp white tablecloth. Festive blooms in plum and burgundy sprang from a little coppery vase – stems shortened to ensure Gideon and I could see each other – and candles, in gold decorative holders, waited to be lit. 'Perfect,' I said. The whole ensemble screamed *l'amour*.

Turning my attention to the oven, I checked the delights within. I frowned. While my mouth drooled at the liquorice-like aroma emanating from the tarragon-infused carrot, mushroom, and hazelnut tart, my eyes struggled with what they saw. Just like my hair, my dish looked nothing like how it was supposed to. 'Remember, it's all in the tasting,' I said, refusing to be disheartened.

It was not my usual fare: I'd have been happy chucking something into the air fryer, but that night I was taking Erin's advice and going all out. Life had been all work and no play for Gideon for far too long and I was determined to show him what he'd been missing. His only job was to pick up the wine.

My phone vibrated in my pocket and pulling it out, I paused, tempted to ignore Erin's incoming video call. I knew she wouldn't be able to help herself. In discussing the best way to approach my date night, she'd already suggested I was a three-bedroomed semi that needed a bit of a facelift, and Gideon was a prospective buyer. As appreciative as I was for her help, that wasn't quite the vibe I was aiming for. On a personal level, Erin had no time for matters of the heart, although while she'd never admit it, I suspected that was because hers had been broken.

I looked around the room again and knowing none of my efforts would have come to fruition were it not for Erin, I sighed. Feeling guilty, I answered her call.

Erin's jaw dropped and she stared at me, agog. 'Blooming heck, it's Mrs Trunchbull.'

I put a hand up to my hair. 'I was trying something new like you suggested.'

'Well don't do it again. It looks awful.'

'Thank you very much!' I let out a laugh. 'Someone's in a good mood.'

Erin's shoulders dropped. 'I'm sorry. Ignore me. I've just come out of a long and somewhat infuriating meeting. I'm starving and you know what I'm like when I'm hangry.'

Boy did I. I'd never forget the time we went for dinner at an Italian restaurant.

Erin had missed lunch and had a difficult day then too. The daggers she gave the poor waiter as he placed her lasagne down on the table. 'I thought this place served traditional food!' she said. Demanding to know why her meal was devoid of béchamel sauce, Erin clearly found the proffered version offensive and while the poor young lad stuttered trying to come up with an acceptable response, Erin verged on crying into her plate.

I didn't know who evoked the most pity. The waiter or my friend.

'These hot flushes aren't helping,' Erin continued. 'You might be young and carefree now, Hattie, but just you remember, you'll be my age before you know it. This perimenopause malarky wreaks havoc on a woman. Rule number one, always wear layers.'

When Erin went on one of her hormonal rants, I'd long learned the best thing I could do to help was let her vent.

'Today's was a corker. My whole being was melting. And you know what men are like. They have zero understanding. You'd have thought I'd asked everyone to line up and jump out of the window, not open the damn thing.'

'And did they? *Open* it, I mean.'

'After some gentle persuasion, yes.'

I struggled to imagine Erin being gentle over anything.

'I said if they refused, I'd be stripping down to nothing but my birthday suit. At which point they were fighting to let the cold air in. I've never seen a bunch of men move so fast. No doubt, I'll be getting a call from HR on account of somehow triggering one of them.' Erin laughed. 'Fingers crossed, it's Callum. The telling off would be worth it. Anyway, I'd better go. My hormones are raging just thinking about it all.'

'Erin?' I said, before she hung up.

'Yes.'

I raised an eyebrow. 'Did you call me for a reason?'

'I did.'

'And that reason was?'

'Good question. I'll text you once I remember.'

I chuckled.

'Something else you have to look forward to,' Erin said. 'Brain fog.' Her face lit up. 'That was it. I called to wish you luck.'

My smile continued. As overbearing as Erin could sometimes be, her heart was in the right place. 'Thank you. For everything.'

'Not a problem. Now you go and sort your hair out.'

No sooner had Erin disappeared, my phone rang again. Seeing it was a voice call from Gideon, I put him on loudspeaker. 'I take it you're in the drinks aisle?' Retrieving a couple of glasses from the cupboard, I carried them over to the table. 'I'm thinking either a Chardonnay or a Pinot Noir.'

'Yeah, about that...'

Placing the glassware down, my smile vanished.

'I've got to work late.'

Telling myself my boyfriend had to be joking, I plonked down into a dining chair. 'Tonight's date night, Gideon. We agreed. You even put it in your diary.'

'I know. But what can I say? It's not like I'm happy about it either. I mean, do you really think I'd still be here if I had a choice?'

The number of hours Gideon spent at the office of late, I was starting to think yes, he would. 'And what about us? Do we even figure in your list of priorities?'

'You know we do. But most people don't have the luxury of being their own boss, Hattie. We can't all come and go as we please.'

I screwed up my face wondering why he was so het up. I was the one being let down. 'What? I'm supposed to feel lucky Gran died now, am I?'

'No. Of course not.' Gideon sighed. 'Please, I'm sorry. That came out wrong.'

Despite my protests, I couldn't deny Gideon had a point. Compared to many, I was fortunate. Ever since Gran taught me to knit as a child, I knew I'd have a job for life. For years, she and I fantasised about me taking over her little wool shop so she could enjoy her dotage, and while Gran might have left her retirement too late to see our plans through, I was still living a version of our dream. I didn't even have a commute. Come five o'clock all I had to do was lock up, turn the door sign to closed and head upstairs to my flat.

'We're meant to be decorating the tree.'

'I'm not stopping you from doing it.'

'And dinner's all but ready.' I took a deep breath and slowly exhaled. He didn't sound like it, but surely Gideon had to know how important that evening was. To me and to our relationship. 'I suppose I could save you a plate.'

'Don't worry. I'll grab something on my way home. We can eat together another night.'

I cocked my head, unable to believe what I was hearing. 'You mean you're not coming over at all?'

'After a long day like today I wouldn't be much company.'

My gaze went from the oven to the beautifully laid table, through to the dimly lit lounge where flames danced in the hearth. Wriggling in my seat, I again felt my new knickers sitting awkwardly. Releasing my trapped skin, I was damned if all my efforts and discomfort were going to be for nothing. 'I could run you a bath,' I said, practising my come-to-bed eyes. 'A relaxing soak would be the perfect wind-down.'

Gideon let out a hollow laugh. 'I've always been more of a shower man.'

'Not a problem.' A delicious smile spread across my face and my tone turned sultry. 'Play your cards right, and I might join you.'

'Honestly, Hattie, as tempting as you think that is, it's gonna have to be a no.'

My shoulders slumped. 'Spoil sport.'

The romantic bubble I'd spent hours creating finally burst and I fell silent. Sitting there in fancy underwear while offering myself up no longer felt flirtatious. It felt humiliating. I should have known Gideon wouldn't play along. He probably didn't know how to. In all the time I'd known him, banter of any kind had never been his thing.

Unless Erin and Joyce are right, I considered. *And I do need to heed Gloria Chalmers's warning.* Despite poo-pooing their suggestion that Gideon could be having an affair, as I chewed on the inside of my cheek, I couldn't help but wonder if my friends were right.

'Look, I've got to go,' Gideon said. 'I'll speak to you tomorrow, yeah?'

Desperate for some sort of reassurance, I opened my mouth to speak, but as kept happening of late, Gideon ended the call before I could utter a word. I stared at my phone, taking in the happy photo of me and Gideon that filled its screen. I ran my finger over his beaming smile. *He wouldn't,* I silently insisted. *He couldn't.*

Turning my attention back to the room, I rose to my feet ready to unlay the table.

CHAPTER 6

Thanks to Gideon's no-show, I'd spent the night tossing and turning. My brain had gone into overdrive, dissecting every conversation Gideon and I had had over the last couple of months. Analysing every word for clues regarding his fidelity, like an emotional pendulum my thoughts kept swinging first one way and then the other. One minute, yes, he was being unfaithful. What other explanation could there be for his distancing? In the next, he wasn't. Gideon was too honest for that.

To quieten my mind, I did what I always did when I had a problem and couldn't sleep. I stopped thinking about it altogether, got up and set about cleaning. Keeping myself busy had always been therapeutic and by 9am when it was time to open The Knitting Nook, I'd scrubbed, bleached and polished the whole of my flat until it shone. Goodness knew what my neighbours must've thought about the early morning vacuuming.

Once I'd opened up downstairs, I spent the rest of the morning tidying the shop and at almost lunchtime I could finally stand back to admire my efforts.

Row upon row, one on top of the other, every ball of wool now sat perfectly aligned. Pattern files stood to attention, organised according to yarn, project type, man, woman and child. After finding the perfect attention-grabbing spot near the entrance, the Christmas gifts I'd ordered were now in full display. I let out a satisfied sigh. Whether they wanted them for their own stockings or someone else's, I knew my regulars would find the little cross-stitch kits, DIY macramé sets and make your own finger puppet selection as irresistible as I did.

I looked out onto the street and, my heart melting at the sight that met me, it seemed I, at last, had a reason to smile. Alex, well over six foot, looked like a gentle giant next to the little old lady he helped across the road. Carrying her two-wheeled shopping trolley in one hand, his other rested against the lady's upper back. He was clearly happy to go at the lady's slow and measured pace and his kindness in guiding her to safety struck me. The two of them chatted as they went; a conversation that continued once they reached the other side. Alex passed the shopping trolley back to its owner and I couldn't help but smile as they said their goodbyes and went their separate ways. Settledown was a world away from the city with its bright lights and fast pace, and Alex appeared to fit right in with the gentler way of living.

My stomach rumbled, reminding me I'd missed breakfast on account of not wanting to mess up my newly pristine kitchen. But with twenty minutes still to go before I could close for my lunchbreak, food would have to wait. Glancing around in search of something else to occupy my mind, my eyes fell on the till and the crochet project I was working on. However, with thoughts of Gideon re-emerging in my head, I wasn't in the mood. I'd only make a mistake and ruin it.

Taking my seat at the counter, I yet again insisted the very idea of Gideon having an affair was laughable. The Gideon I knew had never as much as broken a speed limit let alone someone's heart. He never socialised unless it was a works' do. The few friends he had were back in his hometown and the mere suggestion of going out clubbing would bring him out in hives. Thanks to his disdain for dating apps, Gideon had neither the will nor opportunity to do the dirty. If I hadn't contacted his office for assistance after Gran's death, he'd never have met me. The only chance he had to meet *anyone* was through his job.

A picture of Julia popped into my head and as my uneasiness snapped back into focus, I recalled the previous December when Gideon had first introduced me to his colleague. It was at his office Christmas party, and outside screens or magazines, I'd never seen a woman so glamorous. She put the rest of us in our more casual attire to shame with her coral flutter-sleeve jumpsuit and gold high-heeled sandals. Her make-up was striking and unlike my recent and rather disastrous attempt at a chignon, her lustrous raven updo was styled to perfection.

I frowned. Realising Gideon had yet to mention that year's upcoming office shindig, and I wondered if I should?

The shop doorbell rang and I was glad of the interruption. Wills Patterson burst in from the street bringing a blast of cold air with him. I pulled my cardigan tight across my chest.

'Thank goodness I caught you,' Wills said. 'I thought you might be shut for lunch.' He put a hand up to straighten his windswept hair, but thick and wiry, his follicles appeared to have minds of their own. After every sweep they sprang back up into their original position. 'I was just ribboning Mable's dressing gown, and I ran out of thread, can you believe?'

Very much able to, I smiled. Wills had been the costume designer for Settledown's am-dram group Dramarama since forever and I'd yet to experience a production of theirs that didn't involve at least one haberdashery emergency. This was

Wills's third such visit in as many weeks, so their *Pirates of Penzance* inspired pantomime was proving no different.

Wills headed for the cotton display and perused the reels. 'So how are things with you and your gentleman friend?'

Unfortunately, Joyce wasn't the only one to enjoy a bit of hearsay. Aware that most Settledowners, including Wills, had an inquisitive streak, I knew better than to fall for his casual enquiry. 'Fine, thank you.'

Also like the others, he wasn't one to give up. 'It's just that we haven't seen him around much lately.'

By *we,* we both knew he meant the whole town.

Settledown was a great place to live. Big enough to provide residents with all the necessary amenities, such as a bank, a grocery store, and a doctor's surgery. Yet small enough to maintain a village-like way of life with a real sense of community. But while it was comforting for everyone to know everyone from a safety point of view, that came at a cost. Usually in the form of gossip.

'It's a busy time of year for him,' I said, regurgitating Gideon's claims. 'What with tax deadlines, year-end reports, and new accountancy stuff to get his head around.'

Wills made his cotton choice and, fixing a smile on his face, brought it to the counter. 'That sounds...' He contemplated a moment. 'I want to say interesting, but I'd be lying.'

I chuckled. Having listened to Gideon wax lyrical about assets, balance sheets and accruals, I couldn't disagree.

'It wouldn't do for us all to be the same though, would it?' Wills said. 'Some people love playing with figures, equations and wotnots. Then there are those like you and me, who enjoy working with our hands.'

Again, I wasn't about to argue. For me, anything mathematical was done purely out of necessity.

'It makes me wonder what you and your young man find to talk about, being such opposites.'

Wills launched into a speech about creativity versus logic and as my confusion over Gideon's relationship status with Julia again reared its head, my brain stopped listening. A stab of jealousy pierced my chest as not only was she gorgeous enough to lead even the most loyal of men astray, she had to love number crunching as much as Gideon did. Why else would she be an accountant?

I pictured the two of them sharing a sandwich and some numerical joke that only fellow accountants could understand and while Julia threw her head back in laughter, my boyfriend admired her beauty. I felt a sudden urge to go and catch the two of them out. 'If you must know, we have a lunch date.'

'Sorry?' Wills looked at me confused.

I blushed. He had clearly moved the conversation on. 'Me and Gideon,' I replied trying to sound casual. 'I'm meeting him at his office. Of course, by the time I get there it'll be a late lunch but...'

'You're closing the shop?' Wills appeared surprised. 'For a whole afternoon.'

Despite not having said that, I let his exaggeration pass.

'Then again why not?' Wills continued. 'When you're young and in love throw caution to the wind, that's what I say.'

I wished my reasons were as simple as that.

'I told Martin he was wrong. That the two of you hadn't broken up.'

Ringing his items up on the till, I jerked my head. 'Excuse me?'

'Now I know what you're thinking. That Martin and I have been tittle-tattling. Well rest assured, nothing could be further from the truth.'

I scoffed, aware that what Wills should have said was *nothing could be nearer to the truth.*

'We're just concerned friends. Looking out for a fellow Settledowner.' He turned his attention to the crochet project I'd been working on. 'This is beautiful. You have such talent, Hattie.'

His quick change of subject didn't go unnoticed. Nor did the fact that he was loitering despite my claim I was about to go out.

He ran his fingers over the single and double crochet design, while I checked my watch. 'It's so delicate and intricate. Maybe I should join your club? Learn how to do this myself.'

'I'd be more than happy to teach you,' I replied, while he, at last, fiddled in his pocket for some cash.

'Hattie, we all know that gathering of yours has more to do with bottles of vino than skill sharing. It's not a crochet club; it's a wine club. Probably mulled this time of year.' He chuckled at his own joke. 'Anyway, Joyce and Erin wouldn't know one of these...' He picked up my crochet needle. 'If it poked them in the eyes. What's it going to be anyway? Another fabulous top? Oh, I know, a party dress?'

'A baby blanket. For Ruby Wentworth's little one when the time comes.'

'Oh, that poor girl.' Wills's face crumpled. 'I still can't believe that cad would desert her like that.'

The last thing Ruby needed was anyone talking about her and, eyebrows raised, I stared at him. 'I thought you didn't go in for gossip?'

'You're right.' As if remembering himself, Wills straightened himself up. 'I don't. That was naughty of me.' He finally handed over his money and retrieved the reel of cotton. 'I'm just glad things between you and that man of yours are still good.'

'Like I said, I have a lunch date to get to.'

'Oh, yes. Don't let me keep you.'

I stepped out from behind the till.

'I wouldn't want to get in the way of romance.' He gave me a knowing wink, despite knowing nothing at all.

I refused to discuss my relationship any further and ushered him to the door.

'Say hello to him for me,' Wills said, as I eased him out into the street.

'Happy sewing,' I replied.

Locking the door behind him, I flipped the open sign to closed and hastened upstairs to get ready.

CHAPTER 7

Despite wearing my bobble hat and mittens, I was freezing, but as I crossed my woollen clad fingers and whacked on the van's temperamental heater, I was met with a cold blast of air. 'Please, Beryl, don't do this. Not today.' She evidently couldn't hear me over the sound of her engine and with no warmth whatsoever coming through, I turned the heater off again.

Gideon was forever complaining about my van's rumbling. He constantly badgered me to take Beryl to a garage, but I'd always had more important things to do with my money. Buying stock for the shop, food and paying my electric bill had to take priority. However, as I chugged along, willing Beryl to go faster, I wished I'd taken Gideon's advice. The drive to his office seemed to take forever.

My resolve waned and I wondered if I was being irrational. If I should simply wait until our next date night to talk to the man; have a heart-to-heart about my concerns.

Gloria Chalmers tried that, Gran reminded me. *And look where it got her.*

I considered Gran's words for a moment. 'You're right,' I said.

'Better to know the truth sooner rather than later.' Pressing my foot down on the accelerator, I put pedal to the metal, willing her forward.

Beryl, the only vehicle I could afford after Gran passed, was stubborn and she refused to go anywhere near the speed limit. Not that my impatience helped the journey. Unlike Beryl, my imagination over Gideon and what he was up to readily went into overdrive.

Inhaling and exhaling to control my rising pulse, I tried to force my inner pendulum back the other way by insisting Gideon was as faithful as a puppy and instead of being irrational, I should turn around and go home. I tried to reassure myself that the only reason I'd questioned his fidelity was because of Erin's quip about him *getting it somewhere else* and Joyce's talk of Gloria Chalmers. But it was no good. My friends' suggestions had obviously attached themselves to my brain's frontal lobe and no matter how much I tried to shake them off, they clung on for dear life.

A flurry of images invaded my mind. Discreet glances between Gideon and Julia in team meetings. Close encounters in the stationery cupboard. Romantic meals and hotel getaways. Anxiety threatened to overwhelm me. In my head, the two of them were all but married.

Bang! Beryl backfired, jolting me back to reality. 'Thank you,' I said, clearly needing that as much as Beryl did. Noting I was almost at Gideon's office, I knew, whether I wanted to or not, I couldn't cut and run. If only for my sanity, I had to see things through.

While Gideon might not see Beryl drive onto his firm's car park, everyone in the building would certainly hear her and, determined to keep the element of surprise, I pulled into a space a couple of streets away. Keeping my hands on the steering wheel, I took a moment to steady my nerves. 'You've got this,' I said, at last, grabbing my bag and climbing out.

As I set off walking, my apprehension grew with every step. I'd never turned up at Gideon's office unannounced before and didn't have a clue how he would react. I stopped for a second to check out my reflection in a shop window and pulling off my hat, stuffed it into my pocket and titivated my hair. My gaze drew downwards. 'Bugger!' Taking in my trainer clad feet, I cringed. I was wearing odd socks.

Setting off again, Gideon's office soon came into view, and as I approached, I took a deep breath. 'Whatever happens,' I told myself. 'Just play it cool.'

Making my entrance, I held my head high. Having been in the building numerous times when Gideon had helped me sort out Gran's accounting, I knew where to find him, and I raised my hand ready to push on the plate glass doors that led down an internal corridor.

'Can I help you?' the receptionist asked, stopping me from going any further.

I turned to look at her.

Tinted brows raised, her red-lipstick smile seemed more out of politeness than choice. She obviously didn't go in for niceties.

'I'm here to see Gideon Mayhew,' I said. 'But don't worry.' I made sure to keep my tone light. 'I know the way.'

'Is he expecting you?' she asked, her voice firm.

'No, but–'

'Then please take a seat.' She lifted a phone receiver. 'Who shall I say it is?'

I sighed. 'Hattie.' Sauntering over to the faux leather sofa, I plonked myself down. Disappointed I no longer had the advantage of surprise, I cursed the receptionist's gate-keeping efficiency. I scowled at her. She was obviously power mad.

The receptionist put the phone to her ear and pressed a

couple of buttons. Waiting a moment, she drummed her manicured nails on her desk. 'The line's busy,' she said, replacing the receiver. 'You can leave a message if you like?'

Having driven forty minutes to get there and already given my name, I didn't see the point in leaving. 'It's okay. I can wait.'

While the receptionist turned her attention to her computer screen, I scanned my surroundings. My gaze fell on a huge abstract art canvas that hung on the brilliant white wall to my right. Angling my head this way and that, I soon gave up trying to understand it and instead, focused on the five-foot-tall artificial ficus tree that reflected on the white ultra-gloss tiled floor. I wrinkled my nose. Apart from a string of tinsel that lined the edge of the reception desk, there was no sign it was Christmas.

I recalled my very first visit. Back then, everything about the place had seemed modern and slick but looking at it now, it felt soulless and lacked personality. The atmosphere was as cold as the weather outside. I didn't know how the receptionist stomached sitting there all day. Wishing she'd try Gideon's extension again, I'd only been in the space five minutes and had had enough.

The building's entryway automatically swished open, and a motorbike delivery man dressed neck to toe in leather made his entrance. He carried his helmet in one hand and a padded envelope in the other. The receptionist's eyes lit up at the sight of him and as the two of them chatted, mine darted from them to the internal corridor.

Rising, I tried to appear casual. Pretending to stretch my legs, I manoeuvred towards plate glass doors and seizing the opportunity, slipped into the building's inner sanctum. A quick glance back and I was relieved to see my movements continue to go unnoticed and tootling along at pace, I made my way to Gideon's office.

Reaching his door, I could hear him talking and pressing my ear against the wood, I strained to listen, wanting an idea of what I was about to walk in on.

'I'll show you my spreadsheets if you show me yours.'

Hearing Gideon's tantalising tone, I frowned. Unable to remember him ever talking to me in that manner, it was uncomfortable listening. I didn't catch the response, but Gideon's subsequent chuckle told me it was favourable.

'How do you feel about the double-entry method?' he asked.

My eyes widened. This was a side of Gideon I didn't know about.

'If you don't like it, I can always withdraw.'

I put a hand up to my chest. As accountancy conversations went, his was beginning to sound pornographic.

'You're sure you're okay with this?'

With what? Whomever he was talking to might have been, but I wasn't.

'Fantastic.'

Having heard enough, I pulled my ear away from the door and flinging the entrance open ready to catch him in whatever act was taking place, I burst into the room.

Phone to his ear, Gideon nearly jumped out of his seat. Sat behind his huge leather-inlaid desk, his jaw dropped at the sight of me. 'Hattie, what are you doing here?' he asked, his surprise turning to confusion.

He could play innocent all he wanted, but after what I'd just heard he obviously wasn't alone, and I refused to let him get the better of me. I marched over to him, grabbed his chair and with one quick yank, wheeled him out of the way. 'I just wanted to see what you were up to,' I said, as I checked the void where his feet had been.

Gideon indicated the receiver still in his hand, staring at me like I'd lost the plot. 'I'm on the phone. To a client.'

I scanned the room in search of other potential hiding places. Plusher than reception, Gideon's office held a line of bookcases filled with accountancy manuals, while tasteful and bland pieces of artwork hung above a bank of filing cabinets. My heart sank. Unless there was a femme fatale squeezed in a drawer or between the sofa and the wall, I'd clearly got the situation wrong and what I'd overheard was, indeed, a legitimate professional exchange.

Realising my mistake, I closed my eyes for a second. Having made a colossal fool of myself, I wanted the ground to swallow me whole. My mind raced as I tried to come up with a credible excuse for my actions.

With no choice but to take my earlier advice and play it cool, I fixed a smile on my face and spun round. 'A mouse,' I said. I made a point of checking where Gideon's feet had been for a second time. 'A mouse ran under your desk.'

CHAPTER 8

Closing Gideon's office door behind me, I made my way back down the corridor. Head down, every step felt like the morning after the night before. Admittedly, an actual Sunday morning walk of shame would have been preferable. At least I'd have had fun beforehand.

As I skulked along, I cursed myself for my stupidity. Be it on the benefits of fancy underwear, the marital downfall of Gloria Chalmers, or anything else connected to their idea of relationship counselling, I was never listening to Erin and Joyce again. Twice their not so wise words had left me humiliated. No way was I going for a hat trick.

I sighed, aware that as much as I wanted to blame other people for my predicament, the responsibility was all mine. No one had strong-armed me into turning up at Gideon's office. Everything I'd done was of my own free will. The only person I'd told about my visit was Wills, and even then, I hadn't been honest. As for Erin and Joyce, for all they knew I was back in Settledown, safe and sound at The Knitting Nook.

Getting to the end of the corridor, I pushed on the heavy glass doors that took me back into the reception area and despite the excitable chatter, I was too embarrassed to even look at the people gathered at the reception desk as I passed by.

'Hattie?' a female voice called out.

Almost at the exit, I stopped still. Closing my eyes for a second, I cringed, praying it didn't belong to who I thought it belonged to. I fixed a smile on my face and slowly turned. It was clear the gods didn't think I'd suffered enough and for the second time in as many days, I wished I was invisible. 'Julia. How lovely to see you.'

'Isn't it?' Julia's smile didn't quite reach her eyes. 'You look...' Her gaze went from my head to my feet, a fleeting look of confusion crossing her face as she took in my odd socks. 'Erm, well.'

'You too,' I replied. But unlike her I meant it.

If Gideon was having an affair with this woman, a part of me couldn't blame him. She appeared as glamorous then as I remembered. Wearing a wool trench coat, a cream cashmere sweater and a fitted midi skirt, she'd finished her outfit with heels I'd have broken my neck in.

'Does Gideon know you're here?' she asked.

'Yes.' Trying not to think about the show I'd just made of myself, I cleared my throat, forced to bring my voice down an octave. 'I've just left his office.'

We both stood there. Two relative strangers, with nothing and no one in common, apart from Gideon. Obviously feeling as awkward as me, Julia's brain seemed to scramble for yet another ceremonious statement. Mine, on the other hand, was in fight-or-flight mode, leaving me desperate to run away and hide. 'I'll be off then,' I said, as the silence went on a bit too long.

'Yes, of course. That little wool shop of yours isn't going to run itself.'

Outside, the cold immediately hit me. Rummaging in my bag, I pulled out my bobble hat and mittens, and putting them on, hastened along the street, unable to get back to my van quick enough.

I wanted nothing more than to pretend the whole sorry episode with Gideon hadn't just happened, but pictures of him crawling around his office floor with his bum in the air refused to subside. They would be a permanent reminder of my foolishness. Just like the moment Erin spanked Joyce in the lingerie shop, Gideon's search for a non-existent mouse would be a snapshot in time forever imprinted on my brain.

I shoved Beryl's key into her ignition and turned it, but instead of firing up, she coughed and spluttered. Pulling out the key, I stroked Beryl's dashboard hoping to coax her into action, and holding my breath, tried again. The same thing happened and insisting it was third time lucky, I crossed my fingers, willing her engine to catch as I went through the whole process once more. Beryl's cough grew weak until it petered out to nothing.

Having never identified with a van so much, I, too, lost the will to live and closing my eyes, I let my head drop onto the steering wheel. It landed on the horn, but I didn't move. As the beep droned on, I no longer cared who heard or saw what.

osie Bellridge approached the till with a pair of children's plastic knitting needles and a ball of yellow double-knit wool.

'Let me guess,' I said. 'For Charlotte?'

Out of all Josie's children, Charlotte was the one who stood out. Not because she was cuter or more boisterous than her siblings, but because yellow was her favourite colour. By all accounts, her bedroom was yellow. Her favourite foods were yellow. From head to toe, everything she wore had to be yellow. Charlotte was a chattering, singing, dancing and skipping beam of sunshine.

'She's been nagging me to teach her for a while,' Josie said. 'Today's the day.'

Josie was a fabulous wool crafter. Be it knitting, crochet or needle felt, she made the most beautiful creations and I was pleased to hear her skills were being passed on to the next generation. Although, thanks to her six children, I didn't know how Josie found the time, energy or patience for extras like knitting lessons. Not that you'd know she was the mother of a brood. Josie was efficiency personified and so calm with it. In her shoes, I'd have been a frazzled mess, walking around with bags under my eyeballs. She was clearly made of sterner stuff.

'It's all in the routine,' she said, as if reading my mind. 'And the odd Valium.'

I chuckled. 'Well good luck,' I said.

As Josie picked up her purchases, the shop bell rang, and we both glanced over to see Alex enter. He nodded our way and began perusing the wares, while we soaked up the sight of him.

Josie leaned in. 'Who is *that*?'

The way Settledown operated, I was surprised she hadn't heard. 'The new barman at The Royal Oak,' I whispered.

'I need to get out more,' Josie said, continuing her observations. 'I've obviously died and gone to heaven.' She sighed, wistful. 'I should leave. Before my ovaries start dropping eggs.'

Alex stepped forward and swiftly opened the door for her.

Ducking under his arm, Josie glanced back at me and putting a hand up to fan herself, pretended to swoon. 'Enjoy,' she mouthed.

'Happy knitting,' I said, watching her go on her way.

'Nice sweater.' Alex grinned as he approached.

I looked down at the giant Christmas pudding emblazoned across my front. 'I can give you the pattern if you like?'

Alex's smile continued. 'Some things are better left to the experts. Although I do need some wool.'

'Then you've come to the right place.' I raised an eyebrow, smirking as I gestured to the rows upon rows of available stock.

Alex shook his head. 'Very funny.'

'What kind of wool are you talking about?' I asked.

Alex wrinkled his nose and shrugged. 'I'm thinking grey. No wait, blue.' He placed his hands on the counter. 'Maybe greyish blue?'

'Chunky? Double-knit? Arran? Merino?'

'Now you're just showing off.'

I chuckled.

'To be honest, I didn't ask. It's to send to my Grandma. First, she tells me she's knitting me a scarf for Christmas, then insists *I* buy the wool. Savvy or what?'

I let out another laugh, liking the sound of the woman. 'Cashmere it is?' Moving towards the shelves, I paused. 'Unless you're vegan?'

'Nope.' Alex looked at me confused. 'Why? Does that matter?'

'Never mind.' I scanned the available options. 'This one's nice.' I handed him a ball. 'I must warn you cashmere's expensive. But it's perfect for the job. Not only is it the one of the finest and softest of wools, it's also the warmest.'

As if assessing its texture, he squeezed and caressed the yarn; actions I found distracting.

'And it's durable,' I said, my voice cracking. 'Like I told you, it's not your cheapest option, but your scarf could easily last ten years if you take care of it properly.' The room suddenly felt hot and after one yarn caress from Alex too many, I snatched the wool from him. 'My gran was forever knitting stuff for me. Hats, jumpers, you name it, she used to make it.'

'Used to?'

'She passed away. Eighteen months ago, now.' As soon as the words were out, I could have kicked myself. When it came to the laws of general chitchat, I'd long learned that the death of a loved one was a conversation stopper.

Alex rolled his eyes, proving himself an exception to the rule. 'My grandma's not going anywhere.'

I gasped. 'You can't say that.'

'Why not? It's true. You'd say the same if you met her. She has a severe case of FOMO. No way is she gonna miss out on what the rest of us are up to. She'll outlive us all. Saying that, Mum and Avery are just as nosey.'

'You have a brother?'

'Sister. She's my twin. Not that we look alike. She got the good genes.' He retrieved his wallet from his back pocket and opened it. 'Here, see you for yourself.' Pulling out a photo, he handed it to me. 'This was all of us last year.'

Taken outdoors, it was a typical family snapshot. There were no Instagram-ready poses, everyone simply grinned at the camera. They all had rosy cheeks and wore wellington boots and winter coats. There was a smattering of snow on the ground and a thatched cottage behind them. 'Is that your mum?'

Alex nodded.

The woman was tiny compared to Alex. She had thick dark hair that was loosely piled on the top of her head, and she wore a thick brown wool overcoat with a floral scarf and Doc Marten boots. She reminded me of Helena Bonham Carter.

'Oh, and look at your grandma.' Glasses perched on the end of her nose, her elbows were tucked in and her hands clasped under her ample boobs. She had the cheekiest of smiles and like Alex's mum, she was short in stature. I looked up at Alex, perplexed. 'Where do you get your height from?'

'Dad's side. They're all giants. Mum and dad are divorced, which is why he's not in this picture. Those are my nieces and nephew.'

I took in the three girls and one boy.

'And that's Avery,' he said.

I tilted my head as I looked at Alex. 'No kidding, Sherlock.' Her height and looks spoke for themselves.

It was clear from the way Alex talked about his family they were close. I liked that. One of the things I missed about Gran was the banter we shared.

'Do you have siblings?'

I shook my head. 'My father's never been in the picture and Mum died just after I was born. Some things aren't meant to be.'

'I'm sorry.'

Growing up, I'd craved a sister. Someone to play with when I was little, and as I got older, to share make-up tips, celebrity gossip and boyfriend highs and lows. We could have danced around our bedroom, sung into hairbrushes and swooned over the latest heartthrob. 'Don't be. You can't miss what you've never had.'

'Must've been hard though?'

'Gran more than made up for it. She did a great job raising me.'

Alex smiled. 'I can see that.' He nodded to the ball of wool in my hand. 'I'll take four of those please. According to Gran that should be enough.'

I nodded my agreement and grabbing another three, I headed to the counter.

'Did you get your van sorted?' Tucking away his photo away, Alex followed me over.

I narrowed my eyes. 'How do you know about that?' I took a deep breath and sighed. 'What was it this time? Smoke signals? Jungle drums? Don't tell me, yodelling?'

Alex laughed. 'None of the above. I saw you in the cab of a tow truck and assumed the vehicle on the back was yours.'

'Poor Beryl,' I said, bagging the yarn. 'I just hope they can fix her.'

Alex looked at me deadpan. 'Beryl?'

'What's wrong with that? It's a lovely name.' I rang up Alex's purchase. 'So how are you settling in?'

'So far, so good. Although I still need to find somewhere else to live. I could probably cope with the noisy renovations. It's the getting roped in for extra shifts when I don't want them that's annoying. One of the perils of being on site.'

'I get what you mean. I'm often down here doing inventory checks when I should be upstairs with my feet up.' I supposed that was the downside to living alone. With only a TV for company most evenings, it was easy to work late and on occasion seemed preferable.

I recalled Joyce's suggestion that Alex could move in with me. At the time I'd thought the idea ridiculous, but not only would the company do me good, thanks to Beryl's breakdown and the huge repair bill I'd no doubt be left with, the extra cash would come in handy. Besides, offering him a place to stay wasn't like putting an ad out and inviting a complete unknown into my house; I knew a little bit about him. I felt safe with Alex; he helped old ladies across the street, for goodness' sake. 'I have a spare room,' I said. 'You can always rent that?'

Alex stared at me surprised.

'I know it's not the same as having your own place, but it would get you out of the pub until you find somewhere more suitable.'

'It's kind of you to offer but...'

'There are no buts from me. If you've got good references and can pay your rent, it's yours if you want it.'

Alex scrunched his nose. 'I can't say I'm not tempted. Although I'm heading home for Christmas, so I wouldn't need it until the new year.'

'Tell you what, why don't I show you the room and we can take it from there? You don't have to decide now. Just know it's an option.'

Alex's face lit up. 'That would be great. As long as you're sure?'

Being truthful, I wasn't sure at all. Especially after the previous day's whim, when I'd had Gideon crawling around the floor looking for a pretend mouse. I obviously wasn't made for spontaneity, but in this instance, thanks to Beryl it was a case of needs must. 'Brilliant. Just let me lock up and I'll take you upstairs.'

Alex stood there dumbfounded, while I headed to the door and flipped the shop sign from open to closed. 'You mean now?' he asked.

'There's no time like the present,' I said, before either of us changed our minds. I gestured the way. 'After you.'

CHAPTER 10

*L*etting Alex go before me, the two of us headed up the first flight of stairs. The scent of his aftershave floated towards me – sandalwood and spices. He smelt gorgeous, and I had a great view of his backside. I knew I shouldn't look, and I kept averting my eyes, only for them to be drawn straight back to it.

Entering the lounge, I hoped Alex hadn't anticipated minimalist white. My taste in home décor was the opposite; it was maximalist, colourful and eclectic. Straightening the burgundy and orange cushions scattered on my green velvet sofa, I felt self-conscious. As if, by extension, I was somehow being assessed as well as my home. Thanks to my early morning blitz, I consoled myself in the fact that it was clean and tidy. 'So what do you think?' I asked.

Alex glanced around at my gilt-framed pictures and antique lamps and line of wall-to-wall, rammed in no particular order, bookcases. He took in the wood burner and its accompanying stone mantel. 'It's very you.'

Following his gaze to my floral reading chair I couldn't gauge whether that was a compliment or not, and I found myself feeling protective of all I surveyed. I loved everything about the place. It was cosy and interesting and yes, very much me.

His eyes settled on my Christmas tree. Far too big for the room and crowded with mix-and-match baubles and all shades of tinsel, it was kitsch and nostalgic and reminded me of Gran. Alex clocked the angel sat on a kitchen chair that I'd dragged through to use as a makeshift ladder. But even that hadn't given me enough height to reach, and I'd left it where it was in the hope that Gideon would do the honours when he finally got round to visiting. The way things were going, it would still be sat there in the new year.

Alex headed straight over and picked up the angel. 'Do you mind?' As I nodded my approval, he climbed up on the chair and easily popped her in place. She seemed to smile down as if glad to finally be where she belonged.

Back on terra firma, Alex took in the magnificent ensemble. 'Perfect,' he said.

I recalled the previous year when Gideon first saw my tree decorations. Rather than praise the mass of gay abandon, he didn't understand it. He felt a more curated approach would have yielded a better result.

I gestured toward the kitchen. 'Shall we?'

As I moved to pick up the chair to take with us, Alex stopped me. 'I've got it.' Carrying it through, he placed it at the dining table that sat under the window. 'This is nice,' he said, looking out into the distance at the rolling countryside.

My heart suddenly skipped, as, for a moment, I thought I saw Gran stood next to him. She loved to soak up that view too. It never failed to amaze her how it constantly altered thanks to moving cloud shadows and the changing angle of the sun. She particularly liked it in winter when the hills were white with snow. Pulling my thoughts away from Gran, I drew Alex's focus away from the window and into the room.

'Obviously I'll clear a cupboard for you. And provide a shelf in the fridge.'

His attention went from the cooking area to me. 'Thank you.'

'We have another flight, I'm afraid.' I, again, let him go first. As I directed him to the bathroom, I hadn't realised how many bubble baths, salts, lotions and potions I had on display. My cheeks burned red as I spotted my underwear drying on the radiator, amongst them the fancy set I'd bought for mine and Gideon's date night.

'Very nice,' Alex said.

My mouth fell open, and I flashed him a look, relieved to see he was talking about the shower, not my choice in lingerie. Seizing the opportunity, while he admired the plumbing, I snatched up my knickers and bras and hid them behind my back. 'And this is where you'll sleep,' I said, encouraging him out of the room completely. Watching him step towards his would-be bedroom, I flung my underwear through my door and closed it.

Light flooded into the white-painted room from a window that replicated the one in the kitchen and offered the same view. Alex made straight for it.

I paid more attention to the rest of our surroundings. The double bed wasn't made up and despite having a dressing table and wardrobe, the room felt soulless compared to the rest of the flat. It lacked personality, much like Gideon's office. The bigger of the two bedrooms, it had once been mine, but to feel closer to Gran after she'd passed, I'd shifted all my belongings into hers. I chewed on my lip, regretting the fact I'd done nothing with the space I'd left behind. 'It's a bit stark now,' I said. 'But once you get your things in here it'll be cosier.'

'It's fine.' Alex turned to me with a smile; the first I'd seen since our flat tour began. 'More than fine actually. It's a good size. It's bright and airy. And that view.' He indicated the window and beyond. 'It's screaming to be put down on paper.' He looked my way again. 'Would it be all right if I set up an easel?'

'You paint?'

'I've been known to. Because of the age of the building, my room in the pub is too dark. It would be great to get my brushes out again, if that's okay with you?'

I smiled, liking the idea of having another creative around the house. 'As long as you stick to the canvas and not the walls.'

'You're not a fan of murals then?'

I gave him a mischievous smile. 'You could draw me like one of your French girls.'

Alex looked at me direct. 'I'm up for that if you are?'

My cheeks reddened. His expression was so serious, I didn't know how to respond.

A smile spread across Alex's face. 'I'm only joking. Unlike Titanic Jack, I've never painted a nude in my life.'

'Glad to hear it.'

He winked. 'Not a Parisienne nude anyway.'

Again, I couldn't tell if he was teasing.

'There is one thing,' I said. 'I have a boyfriend who'll be around from time to time.'

'Oh.' Alex's brow knitted.

'That won't be an issue, will it?'

'Erm, no, of course not.' He raised his eyebrows. 'The question is, will my presence be a problem to him? The last thing I want is to cause any upset.'

'I appreciate the concern,' I said. 'But this isn't his flat, it's mine.'

'Fair enough.'

'Besides, knowing Gideon, he'll be more interested in the fact I've sourced a new income stream.' I pictured him poring over some financial statement. 'Accountants do like a positive cashflow.'

'They do, indeed,' Alex said.

'Plus, he's not the jealous type, even if we are going through a bit of a bad patch.' I scrunched up my face. 'Then again, I'm not sure if we're going through a bad patch at all. I could just be imagining it.' I paced up and down. 'I suppose if I'm completely honest, I doubt he'd ever know you're here anyway. The man's always at work to the point we never actually see each other.' I stood still. 'The way things are, I may as well be single.'

I realised Alex was staring at me and remembering myself, fell silent. Mortified, my cheeks burned all over again. I couldn't believe I'd rambled on like that. 'I'm sorry.' It was one thing spilling my guts about Gideon to Erin and Joyce, but do it with a relative stranger. I waved a dismissive hand and plonked myself down on the edge of the bed. 'I don't know why I said all that. Or where it came from.'

Alex laughed. 'Don't worry, I'm used to it.'

As kind as it was of him to say, I raised an eyebrow, not sure if I believed him.

'Honestly. In a family full of women, I'm everyone's first stop when it comes to advice on men.' He sat down next to me. 'Of course, I'm hoping that'll change when my nephew grows up. It's bad enough knowing what Mum and Avery are going through sometimes. There are things I don't need to know about my nieces.'

I smiled, trying to hide my continued embarrassment. 'Even so, Gideon and I are not your problem.'

'Maybe not. But if you really want to sort things out, my suggestion would be to talk to him. Tell him exactly how you feel and what you expect him to do about it.'

'That's what I thought I'd been doing.'

Alex let out a quiet chuckle. 'We men can be a bit thick when it comes to relationships.'

I suppose that explained why, regardless of how many times

I'd relayed my concerns, the message hadn't got through. 'You're probably right.' Compared to Erin and Joyce's advice, Alex's at least sounded sensible.

'Sometimes you have to spell things out for us.'

I took in Alex's sincerity, wondering if he was talking from his own experience rather than someone else's. Dismissing the idea, I doubted any woman would have to talk to him like they would to a five-year-old. Alex had shown himself to be respectful and kind. Looking into his deep brown eyes, my heart sped up and my body warmed.

Suddenly uncomfortable, I jumped to my feet. 'So what do you think?' I swallowed hard and using one hand to rest my elbow in, I put the other to my chest. I gestured to the room. 'Can you see yourself staying here?'

CHAPTER 11

With the flat tour over and Alex having gone on his way, I wasted no time getting online to check out bedding and curtains for his room. Sat at the till, I scrolled through my phone, determined to make the space less hostel-like. 'Too plain.' My jaw dropped. 'How much?' Trying to find a balance between style and cost was proving difficult.

'Ooh, this is nice.' I zoomed in on a duvet set, admiring the pinsonic design that gave it its quilted effect. Assessing the colours available, I clicked on white knowing it would fit in with whatever scheme Alex chose for the rest of his personal space. Checking the price, it was a little more than I'd hoped to pay, but unlike some, not too much over. Adding it to my virtual basket, at least my soon-to-be lodger wouldn't think I was cheap.

I looked up from my mobile with a satisfied sigh. When Joyce had suggested I take Alex in, I'd thought it an absurd idea. But that lunchtime's flat tour established I'd been right to change my mind and offer him a room. Alex would make a great flatmate. He was funny and charming and...

Good looking, Gran said.

'Which has got nothing to do with anything,' I replied.

Plus, he's a great listener. The naughtiness in her voice was undeniable.

My stomach lurched. 'Thanks for reminding me.' I couldn't believe I'd launched into a rambling woe-is-me session. When he moved in, Alex would be my tenant. Not my own personal agony uncle.

I pondered his advice, wondering if Alex had had a point. Though I thought I'd been clear with Gideon, the fact that nothing had changed between us showed I hadn't been clear enough.

You need to tell him you deserve better, Gran said.

Swiping my phone screen, I came out of the internet and brought up Gideon's number. I chewed the inside of my cheek as I contemplated calling him.

You're not a toy he can just pick up and put down at whim, she said.

As I pictured Gran's stern expression, my mind drifted back to my youth. Back then, Gran was forever telling me that when the time came, I needed to find a man like my grandfather. In her view, not only was he the best partner a woman could have, he was a great dad. I might never have got the chance to meet him, but thanks to Gran's memory sharing, I felt like I knew him.

He'd been the love of her life. Funny, smart and ever so handsome, and according to Gran, also quite the romantic. He regularly came home with flowers for no reason other than he thought she'd like them. He'd pen little poems for her and wasn't afraid of public displays of affection. 'It's the little things that count,' Gran would say.

She kept two photos next to her bed. One of my mum and one of him. I often heard her talk to the picture of my grandfather. She'd chat to him about her day, update him on my latest news, and she didn't only tell him how much she missed him, she'd scold him for leaving her without a moment's notice, as if his heart attack had been a choice.

At the time, I thought it strange how she never gave my mum's photograph the same attention. Even in conversations with me, Mum seemed to be a no-go subject. Heck, it didn't matter how many questions I asked, there was always some excuse as to why we couldn't talk about her. Gran was too busy. Gran was too tired. Gran couldn't remember. It was only when I came home early one Wednesday afternoon that I understood why.

I recalled hearing Gran's harrowing cries as I'd headed up to my room. Pausing on the landing, I'd crept towards her doorway, instinctively knowing I had to keep out of sight. I peered through the gap, to see her rocking back and forth, releasing wail after wail of face-contorting, gut-wrenching pain. Seeing the photo of Mum clutched tightly to her chest, that's when I knew that the loss of her daughter was too painful for Gran to contemplate. I never tried to discuss Mum again.

Still feeling the absolute devastation of Gran's grief, tears ran down my cheeks and shaking myself free, I wiped my eyes, returning my thoughts to her happier memories. These always involved my grandfather and were the reason she never sought a second chance at romantic happiness. Like Gran often said, no man could ever compare and, just like she insisted I should never settle, neither would she.

What would she think of my relationship with Gideon? Ours wasn't filled with a Hollywood-style passion, but in reality, I didn't think many were. At least not where I lived. In my little town couples tended to rub along, not set each other's hearts on fire.

But did they start out that way? Gran asked. *There's a difference between settling into a deep and loving companionship and accepting second best.*

I sighed. Gran had a point.

Which camp do you and Gideon fall into?

It was a question I didn't know how to answer.

Chatter outside the shop window caught my attention and craning my neck I looked out to see Aggie Johnson and Tori Smith revelling in an excitable exchange. Frowning, they waved their hands as they talked, and repeatedly pointed to the bookshop next door. In their forties, the two weren't just avid readers; they were literary snobs, and probably my neighbour Janice's best customers. I assumed they were complaining about the bookshop not being open for the last couple of weeks because, heaven forbid, they didn't get their hands on the latest must-read Christmas titles.

I sighed. *Christmas.* I'd been so focused on my relationship with Gideon, I'd hardly given the festive season a thought. With less than three weeks until the big day, I still had gifts to buy, a grocery shopping list to organise, and my Yuletide TV viewing to decide on. I chuckled, recalling my annual discussion with Gran as to whether *Die Hard* was a Christmas film.

Of course it is.

I shook my head. 'No, it's not.'

I returned my attention to my phone. A week ago, the mere thought of spending the big day with Gideon made me buzz with excitement. Now I couldn't be sure we'd even be a couple come December 25th. I sighed, realising if we were to have any chance at a merry Christmas, let alone a future, I needed to take Alex's advice and properly spell things out. Even if that meant issuing an ultimatum; either Gideon gave me the attention I deserved, or we were through.

I simply had to one hundred per cent mean it.

That was the thing about final warnings. They were all or nothing. Once said, not seeing it through would be like giving Gideon the go-ahead to treat me how he wanted, because despite any assertion, I wouldn't really do anything about his behaviour. Wondering if I was prepared to risk being on my own, a knot formed in my stomach and my finger hovered over the screen.

Pulling myself together, I asked myself what I was waiting for and hit the call button. Listening to the tone, I swapped my phone from one ear to the other, half expecting Gideon to let it ring out.

'Hattie,' he said, at last, picking up. 'Is everything all right? It's just that I'm in the middle of something.'

Quelle surprise. I rolled my eyes. 'We need to talk.'

'What, right now? Can't it wait?'

'It's not life and death if that's what you mean,' I replied. 'But it is important. I think we need to clear the air on a couple of things.' My words were met with silence and as I waited for him to respond, I glanced out of the window to see Gary Russel from the butchers opposite join Aggie and Tori.

'Okay,' Gideon finally said. 'I could call round to yours one evening.'

The trio's conversation outside my window grew louder and curious, I got up from my seat at the till. Keeping my phone to my ear, I headed for the door and opening it, stepped outside. My eyes widened. The last thing I expected to see was a someone up a ladder, securing a 'For Rent' sign to the bookshop. Janice hadn't said a word about shutting down.

'Hattie, are you still there?'

Turning away from the streetside fanfare, I gave Gideon my full attention. 'Yes, and what I have to say can't wait. I just need you to listen.'

With Ruby Wentworth's baby blanket finished and beautifully wrapped, I made my way down the high street ready to hand deliver it. A festive spirit was in the air and, clocking the number of tourists around, I wondered if it might have been better to open the shop instead. I just as quickly dismissed the idea. After all the recent drama, giving myself a Sunday morning lie-in and enjoying a stroll through town was much preferable. As was sampling the wares on offer at The Beanery.

The Beanery was one of the best cafés around, and I expected to find it busy. A family affair, owned by Ruby's parents Simeon and Natalie, it was the face of their award-winning coffee roasting company. The fact that Ruby was a baker extraordinaire only added to The Beanery's reputation and people came from far and wide just to taste her divine red velvet cake with its decadent chocolate flavouring and dreamiest of cream cheese frosting.

Stepping inside, I joined the queue of customers, using the time to admire Ruby's creations. The display counter was a sight to behold, and my eyes delighted at the fudgy Bundt cake, covered in a rich ganache. While my mouth drooled over the lemon meringue cheesecake with its cracker crust, bright yellow curd and swathe of toasted egg whites, my nose happily overdosed on the aromas of cinnamon, mocha, nutmeg, and ginger. My senses were in dessert heaven.

Ruby had excelled on the Christmas theme thanks to the array of candy cane, Grinch, and polar bear cupcakes. Her pistachio and raspberry Yule log looked divine and her stollen with chocolate chips and marzipan came as no surprise. It had always been a Settledown festive favourite. Ruby's masterpiece, however, had to be the fabulous Christmas tree cake. Green buttercream had been piped to give the illusion of branches, and it was covered in a range of sprinkles that represented colourful baubles. A light layer of powdered sugar created a snow effect. The whole ensemble was ginormous and a huge feat of engineering.

'Hot chocolate with all the trimmings, please,' I said as I, at last, got to the front of the line.

'Coming right up.' Wearing a Santa hat, an apron to protect her clothing from potential spills, and a smile, Natalie set about making my order.

With a mountain of marshmallows, whipped cream and chocolate shavings, I couldn't wait to get my hands on it. It was like a drink and a dessert all rolled into one. 'How's Ruby?' I asked.

'Still pretending she's fine.' Natalie rolled her eyes. 'Throwing herself into work whether she's ready to or not.' She nodded to the Christmas tree cake. 'My case in point. Goodness knows what we're supposed to do with it.'

I chuckled.

'Don't repeat that,' Natalie said. 'Whatever gets her through this is fine with me.'

I reached into my bag and pulled out the gift I'd made. 'Hopefully this will cheer her up.'

Admiring the wrapping paper with its baby bootie print and mint green bow, a grateful smile spread across Natalie's face. 'Please tell me it's one of your creations?'

'A blanket for the baby,' I said. 'She can open it now or if she prefers, save it for after the birth.'

'I can't tell you how much I appreciate this. And so will Ruby.' Natalie lowered her voice and leaned towards me. 'As you can imagine, not everyone around here has been quite so generous of spirit.'

My heart went out to her and her daughter. 'They'll soon find someone else to talk about.' I dug into my bag again for my purse.

'You can put that away,' Natalie said, her expression stern.

About to argue, I could see I'd be fighting a losing battle. 'Thank you,' I said, doing as I was told.

A group of people, trussed up in woolly hats, thick coats and walking boots made their entrance. 'I'll leave you to it,' I said. Picking up my drink, I scanned the room for a table and spotting one in the window, I headed over.

Taking off my coat, I put it on a chair and settled into the seat opposite. I scooped up a mound of marshmallows and spooned them into my mouth. Watching Natalie give the newcomers a friendly welcome, I wondered how she managed to hide all the worry she had running through her head. Despite her daughter's pretence, Ruby had definitely taken her break-up with Liam hard, and as her mother, Natalie's helplessness was understandable. I sighed, unable to properly imagine what either woman was going through. Ruby and Liam had seemed besotted with each other. The perfect couple, in fact. Ruby's situation certainly put mine into perspective.

I considered my call with Gideon and, knowing he couldn't

in any way be compared to Ruby's scoundrel of an ex, wondered if I'd been too harsh. Refusing to let him get a word in, I'd outlined my expectations with no room for manoeuvre on his part. Not that that had stopped him trying to interject.

'But it's a busy time of year... But it's all right for you... How do you know I'm not doing this for us...?'

I, however, was done with excuses and had insisted work or no work, our relationship from that point forward had to come first; he couldn't have it both ways.

I ate a spoonful of cream and stirred what was left until it disappeared into my hot chocolate. Glad that Gideon and I were finally on the same page, I could concentrate on Christmas. Reaching into my bag for a pen, I knew to have any chance at creating the best celebrations ever, I needed to get cracking.

I smiled at the thought of Gran tutting over how slack I'd been on the preparation front. Unlike me who preferred to pick up everything I needed via a single big food shop, she was one of those women who made her own Christmas cakes and puddings, starting in September. Gifts would be bought and wrapped by the time Guy Fawkes night came around, and decorations would be up come December 1st. Gran insisted the weeks running up to Christmas Day were to be enjoyed, not spent running around like a headless chicken. Picturing myself forced to charge up and down the supermarket aisles battling for the last box of stuffing, I appreciated that sentiment. *Thank goodness for home delivery.*

Grabbing a napkin, I spread it out, using it to list all the people I wanted to buy gifts for. *Gideon, of course. Erin and Joyce.* I paused and chewing on my pen lid wondered if, as my soon-to-be flatmate, I should include Alex.

'Mind if I join you?'

I looked up and as if I'd magically summoned him, there he

was. My face broke into a grin. 'Alex. I was just thinking about you.'

Alex gave me a naughty smile. 'Pleased to hear it.'

Chuckling, I reached over and moved my coat out of the way. 'You wish.'

Placing his coffee down, Alex took the proffered seat. 'I can give you some paper, if you'd like?' He took his sketchpad from his jacket pocket.

'No need. I'm only making notes for Christmas which I'll, no doubt, redo when I get home.'

'A serial list maker, eh?'

I laughed. 'As Gran would say, when it comes to Christmas, organisation is key.'

'She sounds like my mother.'

'I'm not surprised with seven to cater for. I feel under pressure with only me and Gideon to think about.'

Alex cocked his head. 'Does this mean you took my advice?'

'I did. I made my point using words with no more than two syllables, and he now knows exactly where I stand. So, thank you.'

'Does this boyfriend of yours know about your new tenant?'

'He does.'

'And is he okay with it?' Alex picked up his drink.

I nodded. 'He thinks it's a great idea. In fact, so much so, he'd like to meet you.'

Coffee cup to his lips, Alex lowered it. 'I'm not sure how I feel about that. Should I be nervous?'

I let out a laugh. 'Not at all. Gideon doesn't want any awkwardness either. I suggested we swing by the pub. Tomorrow evening, if you'll be there?'

'To keep the bar between us should things go awry? Good idea.'

Smirking, I shook my head. 'To get it out of the way.'

Alex winked. 'I'm sure me and this boyfriend of yours will get on great.'

CHAPTER 13

As I made my way to The Royal Oak, I regretted my chosen footwear. The pavement was thick with ice, and in my one-inch heel ankle boots, I kept slipping and sliding. It was a struggle to stay on my feet. To make matters worse, I felt slightly nauseous. Not even the festive comfort of Settledown's Christmas lights and Nutcracker window displays could ease my nerves. I crossed my fingers inside my mittens. Having Alex as a tenant would be so much easier if he and Gideon got on.

As I approached the pub entrance, I scanned the vehicles in the vicinity. Gideon had rung to tell me he was on his way and that he'd meet me there, but there was no sign of his car. The knot in my tummy tightened. *Please don't let me down again.* Entering the building, I checked the time. Much to my relief, Gideon wasn't late; I was early.

From his position behind the bar, Alex looked up from his sketching. His smile grew as he watched me take off my coat. Putting down his pencil, he indicated my outfit. 'Very nice.'

I, too, gave my attire the once over. Hoping to show Gideon what he'd be missing if he didn't stick to his word and put us first, I'd teamed black skinny jeans with a fitted black polo neck and striking gold dangly earrings. I'd pulled my hair into a tight ponytail that sat at the nape of my neck, and I'd even put on a little make-up. The boots I wore might not have been as death-defying as the kind Julia preferred, but for a woman like me who was constantly in flats and had just free-styled along an ice-rink of a street, my choice was death-defying enough. I wrinkled my nose. 'Not too much?' My outfit might have looked great in my bedroom mirror, but in Settledown's Royal Oak on a weeknight, I suddenly felt a tad conspicuous.

'Not from where I'm standing.' Alex gave me a cheeky smile. 'Although if you've changed your mind about me moving in, you only had to say.'

Confused, I jerked my head. 'What do you mean?'

'Why else would you be sabotaging my chances? No way is that man of yours gonna let me have a house key when he sees you like that.'

I grinned. My style usually garnered words like *quirky, individual* and *off-beat*. People certainly didn't give my appearance out-and-out compliments. Alex was just being kind, but I had to admit his words were something of a confidence boost. 'You won't be saying that once you've seen me first thing. My hair doesn't get brushed until after at least one cup of coffee.'

Alex winked. 'Looking forward to it already.' He indicated the various drinks available. 'What will it be? A glass of white while you're waiting.'

I nodded and as Alex set to work, wondered how a man as good looking as him managed to have a personality to match. In my experience, men either had one or the other. A pang of guilt hit me. Knowing how uncomfortable Gideon's relationship with Julia made me feel, should I really be admiring the very man I was about to introduce to him?

Alex placed my drink in front of me. 'You're sure he's okay

with everything? Because seriously...' Again he indicated my appearance. 'I don't think I'd be.'

A cold blast from the entrance hit and we both looked to the door.

'You can ask him yourself,' I said, smiling at Gideon as he came in from the street.

As my boyfriend walked towards us, I watched Alex's demeanour turn serious. A reaction I found sweet; my soon-to-be tenant obviously wanted to create a good impression.

'What's the occasion?' Gideon looked me up and down. 'It's not like you to get dressed up.'

I noted his attire in equal measure. Still in his suit, his tie sat off to one side and his shirt was creased. Remembering how Gloria Chalmers's husband had stopped putting in effort for her on the appearance front, my smile faltered. But refusing to dwell, I counter-argued with the fact that Gideon had come straight from the office.

Alex continued to look uneasy. Anyone would have thought he was attending an interview or meeting his in-laws for the first time, not a flatmate's partner. Not that he needed to worry. Like I'd explained, Gideon wasn't the jealous type. 'Gideon, this is Alex, the lodger I was telling you about. Alex, this is Gideon.'

The two men stared at each other and as the silence between them grew, so did my discomfort. I leaned towards Gideon. 'Aren't you going to say hello,' I said, nudging him into action.

'Yes. Er, sorry.' Gideon cleared his throat and puffed out his chest. 'Pleased to meet you.'

'And you,' Alex replied, deadpan.

Watching them shake hands, I thought Gideon's grip appeared overly firm, and I glanced around embarrassed, hoping no one else had picked up on that. Observing events from his favoured seat, it appeared Ted had and even he, with his farmer's hands, winced. Alex, however, stood his ground.

'Alex is an artist,' I said, desperate to defuse the tension. 'A creative like me.'

Gideon nodded to Alex's sketchpad. 'So I see.'

Embarrassed by his dismissiveness, my cheeks reddened. Gideon might have been a numbers man, but he could have at least pretended he was interested. To make matters worse, Alex clearly recognised disdain when he heard it and picking up his artwork, he moved it out of sight.

Gideon indicated my glass of wine. 'Another one of those please, barman.'

Questioning if Gideon had had a bad day or if he wanted to humiliate me, I leaned into him again. 'You mean "Alex".' I said, keeping my voice low.

'Excuse me?' Gideon clearly didn't care who heard what.

I glared at him. 'I don't know what's going on here, but it needs to stop now.'

Gideon harrumphed.

Placing a second glass next to mine, Alex stood in silence and as my gaze went from one man to the other, their increasing animosity towards each other showed no sign of abatement.

Gideon picked up our drinks and indicated a table. 'Shall we?'

I shook my head, wondering what had got into Gideon. Yes, Alex was tall, dark and handsome; qualities that could be deemed intimidating. But they weren't an excuse for Gideon's behaviour. Julia wasn't lacking in the looks department either, but I'd never once taken out my insecurities on her. More to the point, Gideon would have been furious if I'd tried.

This was not how I'd expected their introduction to go. I looked to Alex. 'I'm so sorry.'

Following in Gideon's footsteps, I watched him empty his trouser pocket of his phone and keys. Placing them on the table, he sat down, leaving me to take the opposing seat.

I frowned. 'What was that all about?'

'I don't know what you mean?'

'I'm talking about how awful you were just now?'

'Was I?' Gideon asked, drinking his wine. 'I didn't realise.'

Refusing to accept that for one second, I glowered. 'You're going to have to do better than that.'

His resolve dissipating, Gideon sighed. 'If you must know, I don't think he should be moving in. I mean, how well do you know him?'

I know he didn't deserve the way he was just treated, I thought. Alex was chatting amiably with Ted. Running through what I'd learned, I knew he was as close to his grandma as I had been my gran. That he was a twin, and his family weren't local. I knew he was a budding artist and had a great sense of humour and a kind listening ear. 'If you must know, not that much. But...'

'So you could be inviting a serial killer into your home.'

'That's hardly likely,' I replied.

'And *that's* not the point.' Gideon again picked up his drink.

I stared at him. In all the time we'd been dating Gideon may have had the odd sulk, but he'd never reacted to any situation like this. 'What's really going on here, Gideon?'

Glass to his mouth, he paused for a second. 'What do you mean?'

'Well, I get that seeing Alex in the flesh might stir up some insecurities.'

Gideon let out a laugh and putting his drink down altogether, he crossed his arms.

'But honestly,' I carried on. 'You're worrying about nothing.'

'You think I'm jealous?' He nodded to the bar. 'Of him?'

'What else am I supposed to think?' I indicated Gideon's defensive demeanour. 'You have to admit, you're being very extreme.'

I wondered if he expected me to be pleased by his response

to Alex. Flattered even. However, aside from the fact that a man like Alex would never in a million years be interested in me, I felt confused by Gideon's disrespect, and ashamed of it. 'As for your thoughts on whether or not Alex moves in, I wasn't asking for your opinion and nor do I need your permission.'

'Well excuse me for looking out for my girlfriend.'

I scoffed. 'Until now, you'd forgotten you had one.'

Clearly we were as stubborn as each other and our conversation reached a stalemate. Hardly able to look at him, I, too, folded my arms. I couldn't believe Gideon had ruined yet another evening.

His shoulders slumped. 'Look, I'm sorry. I'm probably just tired. It's been a long day.'

I shook my head. An apology and an excuse. Talk about covering the bases.

He rose to his feet. 'Let me go and sort things out. I'll get us another drink and we can restart the evening from scratch.'

Watching Gideon go, I wasn't sure I wanted to.

Joyce's words of warning swirled around my head. Just like Gloria Chalmers's husband, Gideon wasn't just lacking in his appearance, he seemed to be causing a problem where there wasn't one. But it wasn't just that. Recalling our bath versus shower conversation when I'd all but offered myself up on a plate, it seemed sexual intimacy was low down on Gideon's priority list too.

I observed his interaction at the bar. As expected, Alex appeared stern. I wouldn't have blamed him if Gideon's words were too little too late.

Diverting my attention, my gaze fell on the belongings that lay in front of me. I supposed on the plus side, *unlike* Gloria's husband, Gideon wasn't keeping his mobile under lock and key. My eyes narrowed as I realised how quick and easy it would be to go through his messages. I knew the passcode; I'd seen Gideon enter it enough times.

The handset seemed to stare back at me, as if enticing me to snoop.

Taking a deep breath, I placed my hand on the table. Breaking into his phone would certainly help clarify a few things. I looked over at the bar again and seeing him still stood with his back to me, I asked myself where was the harm? It wasn't as if Gideon would ever know.

CHAPTER 14

Ready to meet Erin and Joyce for our usual get-together, I approached The Royal Oak. The heat from the mass of bodies hit me as soon as I entered. It was surprisingly busy and the volume of raucous chatter was deafening, the party atmosphere palpable. Taking off my hat and coat, I couldn't help but smile. 'Merry Christmas, everyone.'

Squeezing through the revellers, I was hoping to have a word with Alex. I hadn't spoken to him since Gideon's unacceptable behaviour, and I wanted to apologise and let him know I'd been as infuriated as he must have been. Nearing the bar, a group of young women fawned over him as, to their squeals of delight, he threw a cocktail shaker up into the air and caught it one-handed. He was relishing the attention, so it clearly wasn't the time for a heart-to-heart. Turning around, I went in search of Erin and Joyce.

Fighting my way through to one corner, I was forced to try another. 'Where are you?' I asked. Craning my neck in the hope of spotting them, my friends had to be in the mix somewhere.

'It's a works' do,' Joyce said, when at I last found them. 'Staff from that big office block just outside town. There's a buffet over there if you're hungry.' She picked up a mini quiche from the plate in front of her. 'I can't tell you how good everything is.'

I took in the mountain of food Joyce had availed herself of and decided not to ask if she'd got permission. Although, turning my attention back to the crowd, I doubted anyone would have noticed if she hadn't. The drinks were flowing, and fun was being had by all. 'There's going to be a lot of people suffering hangovers tomorrow.' I pictured the people around me at work the following day, gathered at the water cooler, downing painkillers and rubbing their temples. 'I'm not sure the organiser thought this through.'

'Hark at you, little Miss Prim,' Erin said. 'When I was their age, I was often out until the early hours and still at my desk on time.' She glanced around. 'A couple of paracetamols and a pint of fresh orange juice before bed, trust me, they'll be good to go.'

'It's Alex that I feel sorry for,' Joyce said. 'Today was supposed to be his day off but he's been roped in to help. Again.' A naughty smile spread across her face as she looked my way. 'Speaking of whom...'

'Oh yes,' Erin jiggled her shoulders in excitement. 'What's this I hear about you shutting up shop in the middle of the day and heading upstairs?'

I stared at Joyce. 'Someone's been talking.'

'You're not denying it though, are you?' she replied, biting into a chicken leg.

I picked up the glass of wine that had awaited me. 'I was showing him the flat if you must know.'

Erin narrowed her eyes. 'Is that all you showed him?'

'Yes,' I replied, surprised yet not surprised she'd question otherwise. 'I thought about what you'd said about my spare room. Thanks to Beryl breaking down, I need the extra cash, so it seemed like a no-brainer.'

'Gideon isn't happy with the situation though, is he?' Joyce asked. She, too, picked up her glass.

Pursing my lips to hide my amusement, it seemed nothing got past Joyce. I often wondered if she had a network of spies in and around Settledown or if she operated some heavy-duty surveillance equipment. 'No. He wasn't.'

Erin smirked. 'He suffered an attack of short man syndrome, by all accounts.'

I shook my head at her naughtiness. 'Most men appear short next to Alex.'

'Not that I'm surprised he felt threatened,' Erin said. 'What man wouldn't? Our new barman *is* gorgeous to look at.'

We all stretched our necks trying to get a glimpse of him, each of us frowning at the crowds that blocked our view.

'Regardless, Gideon's behaviour was rude and embarrassing.'

'I bet he's since upped his game though, eh?' Erin said. 'Now he thinks he's got competition.'

I chuckled. For a dedicated singleton, Erin seemed to know a lot about men.

Joyce tucked into a sandwich.

'To be fair to him, once he got over his sulking, he did the right thing and apologised. To Alex and to me.' Although, as much as I wanted to, I couldn't say Alex's presence didn't continue to be Gideon's primary focus that night. 'He also said I was right for insisting we put more effort into our relationship.'

'By *we,* he meant *him* though, correct?' Erin asked. 'And what about this Julia woman?'

I pictured my fingers hovering next to Gideon's phone and how, in the end, I'd snapped my hand back, unable to bring myself to go through with it. I shrugged in response to Erin's question. 'That's something we still need to discuss. He suggested another date night, so I'm planning on bringing it up then.'

'Well that's progress,' Joyce said. 'It's usually you making all the arrangements.'

'Exactly. And not only that, he's taking me out for a change.' For weeks, Gideon had been too tired to do anything but land at mine, eat and then sleep. That's if he turned up at all.

'At least one of us has something positive to report,' Erin said.

'Still having problems with Callum?' I asked.

Erin let out a laugh. 'Funnily enough, he seems to have gone quiet. Which hopefully means he's done with his fun and games.' Her face turned serious. 'It's Mum that's really worrying me. She's acting a bit strange.'

'How so?' Joyce asked.

'She dug out some old letters the other day, from a penfriend she used to have. A French girl, through one of those correspondence exchanges schools used to organise. Hers was a long time ago, as you can imagine. I'm surprised she still had them.'

I took in Erin's concern. 'A trip down memory lane, maybe?'

'Possibly. But I can't help thinking there's more to it than that. Reading them clearly isn't doing her any good. She keeps telling me about how close they were, although they never actually met, and she's got this sad look in her eye. She just keeps saying she wishes they'd never lost touch.'

'That's life for you,' Joyce said. 'It has a habit of getting in the way of things.' She turned her attention to a sausage roll.

'But is that normal for someone her age? Or a sign that something isn't right?' Erin chewed on the inside of her cheek, as if contemplating her own question. 'Plus the lad from next door's still showing his face. Not that Mum sees him as a problem. According to her, she's glad of the company. I mean, what am I? Chopped liver? It's not like I never visit. I'm round there every week.' She took a deep breath and exhaled. 'Anyway, that's enough of that.' Shaking her worries away, she fixed a smile on her face and turned to Joyce. 'So, how are things with you?'

Pushing her plate of food to one side, Joyce wiped her lips with its accompanying napkin. 'I have both good *and* bad news.'

'This sounds interesting,' Erin said, raising an eyebrow.

'Firstly, I took your advice about encouraging Richard on the domestic front and the very next day, I got him to work.'

'Excellent,' I said.

'Depends on how you look at it. On the plus side, he's no longer following me around like a lost puppy.'

Erin gave Joyce a satisfied smile. 'So our words of wisdom worked then?'

'I'll get to that. I'm still on the good news.' Joyce drank a swig of wine. 'Having introduced him to meal prep, it would seem Richard has discovered a love of cooking. He's spending hours finding recipes, learning all about herbs and spices, weights, temperatures, the lot...'

'Impressive,' I said. 'I just cook everything at 200.'

'Me too. Medium if it's on the stove,' Erin said.

'Not only has he taken over shopping duties, giving me even more time to myself, he's banned me from going anywhere near the kitchen.'

'Fantastic,' Erin said.

Joyce sighed. 'That's what I thought too.' She pursed her lips. 'Initially.'

Perplexed, Erin and I waited to hear more.

'Now we have the bad news.'

'Which is?' I asked.

'He's rubbish at it.'

Clamping down on my jaw, I tried not to snigger.

'Honestly, it's like he has zero palate.' Joyce looked from Erin to me. 'Why I ever listened to you two, is anyone's guess. Do you know how hard it is to pretend you're on a diet when you love food as much as I do? Because that's what I've had to resort to. The hours I've spent wondering where the next digestible meal is coming from.'

That explained the mountain of food she'd just waded through.

'It's downright torture.' She glanced over at the buffet table. 'For the love of God, I wish I'd brought a bigger handbag.' She turned back to us. 'I'm really struggling with what Richard puts in front of me. I mean look...' She indicated her torso. 'It's only been a week and I'm already withering away.'

Taking in her fuller figure, neither Erin nor I had the heart to say anything.

'If something doesn't change, I'm gonna die of starvation.' Joyce drank another mouthful of wine. 'If I thought I was going mad before, that's nothing to what I feel now.' She sighed. 'If I've said it once, I'll say it again. It's no wonder couples get divorced after goodness knows how many years. Now I really am on the verge of suggesting it myself.'

'What are you going to do?' I asked.

'You tell me.' She eyed both Erin and me. 'On second thoughts don't. It's because of you two I'm in this mess.'

'At least now you've got space to breathe. Which is what you wanted.' Erin said. 'Every silver cloud and all that.'

Joyce's eyes widened. 'You do know people can *die* from malnutrition?'

One of the things I'd grown to love about Joyce was her flair for the dramatic and unable to hold my amusement in any longer, I let out a laugh. 'You could try telling him how awful his food is.'

'And ruin his fun? Richard is like a pig in the proverbial. I haven't seen him this happy in months. It's like I've no choice but to keep suffering in silence.'

'And eating between meals,' Erin said, nodding to her discarded plate.

'Exactly!' Joyce said. 'I suppose I could do what Janice did.'

'Janice from the bookshop?' I asked. Having seen the 'For Rent' sign go up, I'd wondered what had happened to her.

'Haven't you heard? She went on a pre-Christmas holiday to Cornwall, met the love of her life, and decided not to come back. Of course, in my case I'd be *leaving* the love of mine.' Joyce pondered a moment. 'Or I could save myself the hassle and just kill him before he kills me? Prison food's got to be better than what I'm being served now.'

CHAPTER 15

$\mathcal{I}$'d never been one to sit on my hands, so with Ruby's baby blanket safely delivered, I'd decided to knit some Christmas stockings. I always gave the children of my fellow Settledown traders a handmade festive gift and the pattern I'd chosen was perfect.

The new project had kept my mind occupied, stopping it from overthinking in the run up to my date with Gideon. But as our time together grew nearer, my focus diminished and I found myself wondering why Gideon had organised it.

I looked up from my stitching and stared out of the window, unable to shake off the uneasiness I'd been left with following his behaviour towards Alex. It was after that that Gideon suggested we go out for a change. I'd not registered before how insecure my boyfriend was, and it bothered me to think our upcoming date might be more about him marking his territory than getting us back on track.

Realising there was no pleasing me, I took a deep breath and exhaled. I either wanted Gideon to put in more effort or I didn't. His true intentions would become clear soon enough, and I told myself to give him a chance. Shaking my mind free, I got back to the task at hand.

For an experienced knitter like me, the stockings were straight forward to make and after a couple of days clickety-clacking on my needles they'd been ready to put together. Having spent the morning crocheting their fronts to their backs, I finally reached the very last stitch of the very last stocking. Finishing off to prevent any unravelling, I weaved the length of wool into the design, picked up my scissors and snipped it free.

I spread the stockings out on the counter and admired each one's simple yet individual red, green and white Fair Isle design. I smiled. 'Gorgeous. Even if I do say so myself.' Gathering them together, all I had left to do was stuff the stockings with sweet treats, then wrap and label them. I wrinkled my nose, wondering if I could nip upstairs and collect what I needed before my next customer arrived.

The shop bell sounded, giving me my answer.

I looked to the door to see Karl, Settledown's delivery man, enter. Eyeing the parcels he carried, I fast clapped my hands. 'Wonderful. I've been looking forward to those.'

He clocked my pile of stockings. 'These are nice.' He looked at me, impressed. 'Do you ever put your needles down? Every time I come in you've got something new on the go.'

I laughed. 'It comes with the territory.'

Karl placed his deliveries on the counter and offered his handheld device so I could sign for them.

'How's the family?' I asked, finger penning my signature. 'Lucy normally calls in for a chat, but I haven't seen her for a while? Is everything okay?'

'She's busy getting ready for Christmas. It's our turn to host this year so her parents are joining us. In typical Lucy-fashion, she wants everything perfect. She's got list upon list of things to do.'

A part of me envied her. The opportunity to eat, drink and be merry with a house full of loved ones was something to be cherished, especially at Christmastime. Of course, I knew from experience, the degree of fun to be had depended on the people involved. Celebrating with Gideon's family hadn't exactly been a laugh a minute and the mere thought of returning the favour at my place made me shudder.

'I don't know who's getting more worked up,' Karl said. 'The wife or Alfie?'

My heart warmed. At only two years old, the holiday magic was bound to overwhelm Karl and Lucy's little boy.

'Although after today, I think Alfie might just clinch it.'

I looked at Karl bemused, wondering what could be so special.

'They're off to Santa's Grotto. No doubt, I'll hear all about it tonight.' He rolled his eyes. 'And again tomorrow. And the day after that.'

I chuckled. 'You love it really.'

Karl winked. 'I wouldn't have it any other way.'

The shop bell rang again and seeing Alex come in off the street, Karl stepped back from the counter. 'Looks like it's time for both of us to get back to work,' he said, picking up his device and heading for the door.

'Say hi to Lucy for me,' I called out, making a mental note to knit one more stocking for their son.

Karl nodded at Alex as he passed him on his way out.

'I'm glad you've called in,' I said. 'I wanted to apologise for the way Gideon acted towards you.'

'Not a problem,' Alex replied.

'I wanted to say something the other night at the pub, but I could see how busy you were, what with that office do. I didn't want to unnecessarily clog up the bar.'

'Honestly, don't worry about it.'

'He's assured me he'll be more civil in future,' I said, needing to reiterate my point.

'Good to know.'

I didn't blame Alex for his polite yet curt responses. I doubted he'd ever admit it, but he had to think Gideon was an arse and that I should get rid of him; such thoughts had crossed my mind of late too.

'He's definitely on his best behaviour,' I carried on. 'So much so, he's taking me out for once. I haven't a clue where we're going, which means I don't know what to wear. I just hope I don't embarrass myself and ruin the night before it's begun, all because of the wrong outfit.' Clocking Alex's wide-eyed stare, I fell silent. 'I'm rambling like before, aren't I?'

Alex nodded. 'Just a bit.'

Blushing, I took in his tight expression. Cringing at my insensitivity, I couldn't believe I'd expected him to be interested in any of that. Not after the way Gideon had treated him. 'I apologise. And from now on, I promise to stay clear of any conversation about me and my relationship with you-know-who. We can talk all things Hirst or Koons, or whatever artist you prefer. You could even teach me to draw if you're up for that? Ooh, when you move in, we could do a skills swap.'

'About that...'

'Oh, and these just landed.' I indicated the parcels on the counter. 'New bedding and window dressings for your room. I took note of what you said about liking the brightness in there and knowing that's important, what with you wanting to paint, I went for plain white. The curtains are white too, but they're also blackout, so you don't have to worry about daylight waking you up. Although at this time of year, it's not like the sun comes up early, is it?'

Alex put a hand up to his mouth and coughed.

Pausing, I realised he was silencing me. 'I'm still wittering, aren't I?'

Alex nodded. 'Afraid so.'

I didn't know what it was about Alex that made me lose control of my mouth, but despite saying I'd shut up, the poor man had yet to properly get a word in. 'Again, I'm sorry.' I took a deep breath and bringing up my hands, I placed my palms together and centred myself. Letting them fall again, I smiled at Alex. 'How about I stop talking altogether and you can tell me what you came in for?'

Clearly thinking I was bonkers, Alex regarded me for a moment. 'It's nothing important.' His expression softened. 'I just wanted to let you know Grandma liked the wool I sent up.'

CHAPTER 16

I stared at the pile of clothes that lay on my bed. Choosing an outfit shouldn't have been that difficult, but I seemed to have tried on almost every item in my wardrobe.

Having settled on an ankle-length dress with a flared skirt and flounced hemline, I turned to check my reflection in the dressing table mirror. Its brown fern pattern looked great with my dark green crocheted bolero and black boots, but as I chewed on my lip assessing the whole ensemble, it was clear something was missing.

My face lit up as I realised exactly what that was and opening my jewellery box, I rummaged through its contents. I pulled out Gran's pearl and gold leaf brooch and held it to my chest. 'Perfect,' I said, pinning it in place.

A car horn beeped and I raced over to the window. My chest fluttered at the sight of Gideon's car. I'd tackle the mountain on my bed later and leaving it behind I grabbed my bag and coat, wondering what Gideon had planned for us. I made my way downstairs and through the shop to the street, locking the door behind me. 'You look nice,' I said as I climbed into Gideon's vehicle.

Unlike the shirt he'd worn the last time I saw him, that evening's pale blue number was ironed. His hair looked damp as if he wasn't long out of the shower and I could smell the citrus in his aftershave. For him to go to that much effort, wherever Gideon was taking me, it had to be special. So far, so good. I took a deep breath in anticipation of the night ahead. 'Now will you tell me where we're going?' I asked.

'You'll see.'

My face fell. I hated not knowing what to expect. 'Oh, come on. You know I don't like surprises.'

Gideon rolled his eyes. 'If you must know, I've booked us a table at Zenith.'

'That new place?' I grinned. After weeks of putting work before me, Gideon was certainly making up for it. Zenith was *the* place to eat and from what I'd heard it wasn't cheap. More a saver than a spender, that night was going to cost Gideon a small fortune, even if we went Dutch. I considered my bank balance, hoping it wasn't about to be wiped out. Either way, it was good to see Gideon trying for once, and I leaned over and kissed his cheek. 'Thank you,' I said.

'Don't forget your seatbelt.' Shaking his head, Gideon dismissed my gratitude and, sliding the car into gear, pulled away from the kerb.

The restaurant was located in a neighbouring town and the drive to get there was one of companionable silence. Unlike Beryl, Gideon's BMW was a dream and while he might talk about it in terms of miles per charge and BiK brackets, describing it as a petrol-electric powertrain, I liked the fact it had a working heater and decent shock absorbers. It was great to watch the world pass by in comfort for once.

I stole glances at Gideon along the way. We still had stuff to discuss, like getting to the bottom of his relationship with Julia, and being a realist, I knew depending on how Gideon managed that conversation, the evening could be make or break for us. I wondered if he felt as anxious as I did, but his expression gave nothing away, except that he was concentrating on the icy roads we were travelling.

Finally, we landed, and climbing out of the car, I linked my arm into Gideon's so as not to slip as we crossed the car park. My action seemed to take him by surprise. Understandable, I supposed, considering the way things had been between us of late. Entering the restaurant, my eyes widened. I'd never been in such a gorgeous eatery.

The host took Gideon's name and showed us to our table. Settling into our seats, there was so much to take in. While Gideon perused the menu, my eyes drew upwards to the triple-height arched ceiling from which ginormous chandeliers hung. Lowering my gaze, I took in the modern works of art that adorned the upper walls, and lowering it further, the rich wooden panelling that cocooned the room giving the space a sense of warmth. 'This is beautiful,' I said, soaking up the ambience.

Unlike me, Gideon took our surroundings in his stride. 'Apparently, in days gone by it was the town hall.'

I marvelled at the embowed windows, each one mirroring the shape of the ceiling. 'Most of this must be original. I'm glad the owners didn't rip everything out and start again.'

Gideon scoffed. 'More money than sense, I'd say. Everything was in such disrepair, restoring would have been way more expensive than a complete do over.'

Brow furrowed, I stared at Gideon. He clearly had no respect for architectural history. 'But not half as stunning.' I felt offended on the building's behalf.

'I mean look at that tree.' Gideon indicated a corner of the room. 'It must have cost a fortune. An outlay, I'm betting, has been passed on to us the customer.'

I took in the massive Christmas pine with its coordinated red and gold adornments. Twinkling like the Milky Way thanks to metre upon metre of fairy lights, its tinsel was thicker than some of the scarves I'd knitted. I might have agreed with Gideon regarding its potential cost, but anything less would have looked pathetic and out of keeping. I sighed, wishing that for once Gideon would recognise not everything came down to pounds and pence. I cringed, thinking about my bank balance. The way Gideon was talking, he was definitely going to announce we were going halves.

I turned my attention to the waiters who, in their black waistcoats and white shirts, were efficiency personified. Gliding between tables, they topped up glasses, set down mouth-watering dishes, and chatted with clientele, making sure they wanted for nothing. Like a finely tuned group dance formation, they were graceful and coordinated.

Our table was equally elegant with its crisp white cloth and thick cotton napkins. Our glasses sparkled and I readily imagined a member of staff polishing them until they shone. Silver cutlery galore, I wasn't sure which knife, fork or spoon to use for what, and I glanced at other diners to see how they had tackled my dilemma. I vaguely recalled Gran talking about old-school etiquette, saying something along the lines of 'outside in'. Deciding that was as good a rule as any, I realised people were too engaged in their conversations to notice any faux pas I might make.

I finally looked at the menu. From the risotto, asparagus and smoked salmon to the squash and braised spelt with hazelnut and truffle pesto, everything listed was mouth-watering. Deciding to have the 'catch of the day', the waiter took our order and once again we were on our own.

While I fiddled with Gran's brooch and smoothed down my hair, Gideon played with his napkin. The time for talking had clearly arrived and he suddenly appeared as nervous as I felt. Compared to everyone around us, who amiably chatted non-stop, the silence between Gideon and I grew increasingly uncomfortable and went on for far too long.

'So...' we both said at the same time.

I smiled, pleased that Gideon had recognised the agony of our quietness too. 'You go first,' I said.

Gideon took a deep breath and placing his forearms on the table, clasped his hands. 'I suppose I should begin with an apology for being so distant lately. Work has been hectic.' He swiftly put a hand up. 'I know that's no excuse.' He looked at me direct. 'You deserved better.'

Gideon had been saying sorry for weeks; his pleas had started to seem like lip service. Watching him try to come up with the right words, it appeared he was, at last, taking responsibility for his actions. Perhaps our relationship had turned a much-needed corner and I could finally relax.

'And I shouldn't have behaved the way I did with Alex.' Gideon looked down at his hands as if embarrassed. 'I don't know why I was so rude. It was totally out of character.' He suddenly met my gaze. 'You and I both know I'm not usually like that.' His hands tightened around each other. 'Actually... I do know why.' He swallowed hard. 'It was because...'

My phone suddenly rang from the inside of my bag. Cringing at the sound, I refused to let it interrupt the moment and ignored it. I indicated for Gideon to carry on talking, but the ringtone continued too. Whoever was calling wasn't giving up.

Diners in our immediate vicinity frowned and feeling the weight of their stares, my cheeks reddened at the unwanted attention. Realising I had no choice but to relent, I awkwardly reached into my bag. 'Sorry,' I said, first to them and then to Gideon. I checked the screen. 'It's Joyce.' I dismissed the call. 'She probably wants the gossip on how we're getting on.' Placing my phone down on the table, I gave Gideon my full attention. 'You were saying.'

He gathered himself again. 'I think seeing you so relaxed in Alex's company.' He rolled his eyes. 'Not to mention the way that he looks at you. Well it made–'

'Sorry?'

'What?' My interjection appeared to confuse Gideon.

'Can you just rewind a bit. The way who looks at who?'

Gideon let out a laugh. 'You can't tell me you haven't noticed. He obviously fancies the pants off you.'

I stared at Gideon like he'd gone mad. My phone rang for a second time and again it was Joyce. Irritated, I quickly disconnected her call and went back to focusing on Gideon, waiting for him to elaborate.

'What I'm trying to say, I suppose, is seeing you and Alex *together*...'

I put a hand up to silence him. 'Can I get one thing straight, Gideon. Whatever you think you saw, Alex is not attracted to me, and he and I are in no way *together*.'

Gideon raised his palms. 'Okay, okay. Whatever the situation, it's not like it changes anything. The two of you still got me thinking. About us and about our future.' He rubbed his forehead, evidently trying to control his frustration. 'This isn't going the way I planned.' He composed himself. 'Again, what I'm trying to say is, as couples go, you can't get two people more opposite than us. I'm logical. I work with numbers. Spreadsheets get me excited.'

Recalling the pornographic conversation I'd overheard at his office, that was something I knew all too well.

'And whereas I see the world in black and white, you see a kaleidoscope of colour. You're creative and artistic. And unlike me, a real people person.'

I wondered where Gideon was going with this.

'You've taught me so much and...' He took a deep breath as if steeling himself.

My eyes widened as like a jigsaw puzzle, all the pieces started to fit together. Gideon's jealousy, the expensive restaurant we sat in, the speech he was trying to give. The man wasn't just marking his territory; he was digging a moat around it.

'Hattie...'

I heard myself wince. The room suddenly went quiet and everyone and everything around us faded into nothing. I stared at Gideon, willing him not to say anything else.

Gideon cleared his throat. 'In the eighteen months I've known you...'

Shut up! Shut up! Shut up! I suddenly felt hot and struggling to swallow, I grabbed a glass of water and drank a mouthful. *Please don't do this,* I silently pleaded. Despite demanding more commitment from Gideon, the last thing either of us needed was him getting down on one knee.

'...life has been wonderful. You've...'

My phone rang again and as Gideon fell silent, the two of us stared at each other.

I looked down at my friend's name on the screen. The last thing I wanted was to hurt Gideon, but I knew I couldn't let him finish. I snatched up the handset. 'I'm sorry. I need to get this.'

Muttering under his breath, Gideon threw himself back in his seat, but despite his annoyance, I had to hold firm. There was no way we were ready for marriage and shutting Gideon up was the only way to save his dignity. 'Joyce wouldn't keep trying to get through if it wasn't important,' I said, hitting the call answer button.

'Hattie. Oh, thank God.'

Hearing Joyce's desperation, thoughts of Gideon vanished.

'I'm at the hospital.'

My heart stopped as panic hit me. 'Why? What's happened?' Gideon leaned forward, his eyes questioning.

'It's Richard.' Joyce began to cry. 'I think I'm going to lose him.'

CHAPTER 17

*T*he drive to the hospital was unbearable. Pedestrians appeared as if from nowhere, stepping out in front of us to slow us down. Every traffic light turned red on our approach and took forever to go green.

Joyce had been in too much of a state to speak clearly and my mind struggled to work out what had happened and how. All I knew for sure was that my friend needed me, and she needed me now.

Gideon drove in silence, keeping his eyes on the road ahead, while I sat hands clenched, fingernails digging into my palms. Despite the urgency, Gideon appeared calm and collected. I couldn't tell if he was sulking at me for ruining his big moment, or good in a crisis. Either way, he didn't appear to recognise the severity of our journey and watching him methodically shift through the gears, I wanted to scream at him to put his foot down.

As we neared the hospital, I prayed for Richard to be okay, but a little voice in my head reminded me that such pleas weren't always answered. Refusing to listen, I wasn't giving up hope. Instead, I insisted this time things would be different. They had to be.

At last, we reached the hospital and as Gideon pulled up outside accident and emergency, my hand was already opening the car door.

'I'll call you,' Gideon called out, as I slammed the door shut.

Racing to the entrance, I suddenly stopped. My feet refused to move, and my hands shook. *Come on, Hattie.* I took a deep breath and exhaled. *This isn't about you. It's about Joyce and Richard.* Knowing I had to push through my fears, I pulled myself together and ignoring my pounding heart, charged through the doors. Erin was already at the desk as I fast approached. 'Any news?' I asked, determined not to crumble.

She shook her head. 'Mrs Data Protection here won't tell me anything.'

'I'm sorry,' the receptionist said. 'But like I've explained my hands are tied. Unless you're family, there's nothing I can do.'

'But we are family.' While technically that was a lie, it didn't feel like one. With Gran gone, aside of Gideon, Erin and Joyce were all I had. 'Joyce is our sister.'

The receptionist narrowed her eyes.

Considering the generational age gap between each of us, even I could see how far-fetched that sounded, but with no more time to waste, that was my story, and it was up to her to prove otherwise. 'Our older sister.' Having previously borne the consequence of being fobbed off by a hospital receptionist, I wasn't about to let that happen again and I stared at the woman, eyebrows raised, daring her to challenge me.

'Which makes Richard our brother-in-law,' Erin added, following my lead.

The receptionist flashed Erin a look. 'But you just said...'

We both stood firm, maintaining our position for Joyce's sake.

The receptionist shook her head and sighed. 'You know what, forget it. I'm not paid enough to deal with this.' She indicated the waiting area. 'Take a seat and someone will come and speak to you.' She picked up her phone. 'I'll let your *sister* know you're here.'

The waiting area was packed with casualties and there being no seats left, Erin and I stood off to one side. The place reeked of disinfectant and, thanks to the inebriated brawlers in attendance, alcohol. I glanced around, squirming at the blood that seeped through the bandage on a teenage boy's raised hand. My heart went out to a little girl who, pink and sweating, struggled to breathe as she lay against her mother's chest. There were people wearing makeshift slings while others propped up swollen ankles or sported facial cuts and bruises.

Some, suffering invisible injuries or simply awaiting news like Erin and me, scrolled through their phones. A drunk in the corner burst into song, treating everyone present to a rendition of The Pogues's *Fairytale of New York*.

'That's all we need,' Erin said. 'Like none of us are suffering enough.'

My pulse quickened as I recalled my last visit inside accident and emergency. Gran had tripped outside the shop and by the time Gary Russel the butcher phoned to tell me, Gran was being rushed to hospital by ambulance staff. An X-ray showed she'd landed so hard and at such an angle, she'd broken her hip. When I arrived, demanding they let me see her, Gran was already being prepped for surgery and my pleas went ignored.

My eyes traced the footsteps I'd taken as I'd paced the length and breadth of the area in which I now stood. Alone and in pain, Gran must have been so frightened. Overcome with guilt, I wished more than anything I'd got there sooner to reassure her. To tell Gran how much I loved her. The only life I'd ever known was with Gran and praying like I'd never before prayed, I hadn't known what I'd do if I lost her.

'The two of us against the world,' she would say.

Over and again, I beseeched God, desperate for someone to come and tell me she was okay.

Goodness knows how many hours and a cardiac arrest later, Gran died on the operating table.

I'd previously told Erin about Gran's fate and as if knowing what I was thinking, Erin reached out with a comforting hand. 'Richard will be okay,' she said, rubbing my arm. 'And Joyce is a strong woman. Whatever's going on, she'll get through it.'

I nodded, desperate to believe her.

The doors to the treatment rooms swung open and straightening ourselves up, Erin and I looked over to see a nurse head for the reception desk. Mrs Data Protection pointed towards us and the nurse signalled us over.

'If you come with me,' she said. 'I'll take you through to your sister and brother-in-law.'

Erin and I shared a look, and relieved that Joyce had had the wherewithal to play along with my lie, I told myself that had to be a good sign.

'How is Richard?' Erin asked, as we followed.

'He's suffering from epigastric pain and has an elevated level of pancreatic enzymes which we're treating intravenously. As for his palpitations, his electrocardiogram showed atrial fibrillation, so we'll be monitoring him overnight.'

Listening to the nurse, I didn't understand a word of what she said. All I knew was that Richard's condition sounded serious. Aware the last thing Joyce needed was me breaking down, I did my best to calm myself. Forced to regulate my breathing, I told myself that not everyone goes into hospital and doesn't come out.

'We'll assess him in the morning.'

We turned onto a corridor to see Joyce sat alone and adjacent to a closed door. Her shoulders were hunched, and she fiddled with a tissue so shredded there was hardly any of it left. Nothing like the formidable woman I'd grown to know and love, Joyce looked small and scared, and in that moment, I thought my heart would break.

Clocking our presence, relief appeared to sweep over Joyce, and she rose to her feet and rushed towards us. 'Thank you for coming,' she said. 'I can't do this on my own. And with Nial not being around, I didn't know who else to call.'

'What are sisters for?' Erin said.

The nurse entered Richard's room, leaving the three of us to ourselves.

'The doctor's still in with him,' Joyce said. 'I'm hoping I can see him soon.'

I swallowed hard. 'He's in the right place.' Despite my experience, I refused to think anything different.

Joyce's red and tear-stained eyes began to fill. 'I've never seen anyone in such pain. The way he clutched his stomach and all the moaning and groaning.' Her breath caught. 'I thought he was going to die.'

As Joyce crumpled, Erin and I guided her back to her seat and both of us holding on to her, waited for her crying to ease.

'Do they know what caused it?' Erin asked.

Joyce nodded. 'He's been poisoned.'

Recalling Joyce's prior conversations, I looked to Erin panic-stricken. As we both held our breath, I could see from Erin's expression she was thinking the same thing.

Joyce stared at us, horrified. 'Not by me!'

Erin and I exhaled.

'How can you even think that? He did it to himself.' Joyce reached into her bag for another tissue. 'The blooming idiot went out foraging. You know, being the food expert he is.' She wiped her eyes. 'Great for Christmas, he said, before setting out.' She blew her nose. 'Not only did he come back with a huge bag of chestnuts, he'd already roasted and eaten half of them by the time I got home from town. Except they weren't the sweet chestnuts like the ones you get in the shops.' Joyce sighed. 'All I can say is, thank God he wasn't out collecting mushrooms.'

'So what had he picked?' Erin asked, confused.

Joyce looked from Erin to me. 'The ones you shouldn't eat. *Horse* chestnuts.'

CHAPTER 18

I climbed out of Erin's car and waving her off, watched her drive into the distance until she was no longer in sight. Unzipping my bag, I pulled out my keys and turned to The Knitting Nook. Staring at the entrance, my gaze drew upwards to my living room window. Everything was in darkness and I couldn't face going in.

Struggling to hold myself together, I knew why. Racing to the hospital and seeing Joyce's despair had hit too close to home. It had reminded me of events and emotions I'd spent the last year and a half trying to forget. Stepping into my empty flat would be like reliving the aftermath of Gran's death. I wouldn't just be opening a door; I'd be opening the floodgates that held back my tears.

I dug out my phone, hoping Gideon had called. But there were no messages or notifications on the screen. My heart sank. The last thing I wanted was to be on my own, but without even a text from Gideon to check on me, Joyce, or Richard, making the first move didn't feel right.

Maybe he'd meant to but had fallen asleep? Or maybe he felt too embarrassed after his big moment was cut short? I scolded myself for making excuses. *Or maybe you're just being too kind, Hattie?*

I supposed Gideon's silence was a good thing. If he came round, there was no guarantee he wouldn't pick up where he'd left off and I wasn't in the frame of mind to talk about our future. I was too preoccupied with thoughts of the past.

Putting my phone away again, I tucked my hands in my coat pockets. I looked up and down the empty street and with nowhere else to go, made my way to The Royal Oak. I had no intention of drowning my sorrows, I simply wanted to hear Settledown voices and experience normality. What better place for that than the local pub?

As soon as I entered, my face fell. The place wasn't just quiet, it was abandoned. There wasn't a soul in sight: even Ted's seat at the bar was vacant. Checking my watch, my shoulders slumped. I hadn't realised quite how late it was.

Alex suddenly appeared from a room behind the bar. Jingling the set of keys in his hand, he cocked his head and smiled. 'What time do you call this? I was just about to lock up.'

As he walked towards me, I mustered a smile of my own, hoping he wouldn't notice the tears welling in my eyes. 'No worries.' I turned to leave.

'Hey.' Alex rushed over to stop me from going any further.

Willing myself not to cry, I didn't know if his concern made me feel better or worse.

'I only said I'm closing. Not that you can't have a drink.' He bolted the door shut. 'Come on. Glass of white, is it?'

I nodded, appreciative.

He guided me to the bar and peeling off my coat, put both it and my bag down on a table.

I hoisted myself onto a stool and watched Alex grab two glasses.

'Mind if I join you?' Without waiting for an answer, he filled both anyway and bringing them with him, joined me on my side of the bar.

'Tough night?' he asked.

I lifted my drink and again, nodded. 'You could say that.'

'How is Richard?' Alex appeared genuinely concerned.

'News travels fast,' I said – not that I was surprised word had got out.

'It does when there's an ambulance involved.'

I dreaded to think what tales were already being made up. I smiled. 'He's going to be fine.'

Alex visibly relaxed. 'That's good to hear.' He clinked his glass against mine and we both took a drink.

I pictured Richard pale and weak in his hospital bed while Joyce, with her bloodshot eyes and cheeks drained of colour, eased him forward so she could plump up his pillows. 'He's actually doing well considering.'

'And Joyce? How's she bearing up?'

'She's okay too.'

Alex stared straight ahead. 'And you?'

Until that night, I hadn't realised how much of Gran's death I'd held on to. How, rather than deal with my grief, I'd buried it deep inside of me. I'd focused on practical things like renovating The Knitting Nook and decorating the flat. I'd put time and energy into my relationship with Gideon. What I hadn't done is give myself the emotional space needed to properly mourn and being back at the hospital had brought all my suppressed anguish to the surface. 'I've had better evenings.'

A lump formed in my throat, but I swallowed it down. 'You must think I'm bonkers. One minute I'm whingeing to you about Gideon. In the next I'm rambling on about some ridiculous date. And here I am now about to cry into my drink.' I sighed at how pathetic I must've seemed. 'Tonight just brought it all back. You know, the day Gran died.'

Alex reached out and ran his hand up and down my spine.

'It was so sudden. A stupid fall that shouldn't have led to...' A tear ran down my cheek and I wiped it away. 'Instead of moving in, you should be running for the hills.'

Alex dropped his hand. 'Actually, I wanted to...' He paused, as if not sure he should continue.

'Go on,' I said, thinking he should.

'Forget it. It doesn't matter.'

'Alex, you've started so you may as well finish.'

He twisted his glass between his palms. 'I'm just not sure it's a good idea.'

With him needing to be out of The Royal Oak in a couple of weeks and me in need of the extra cash, I'd thought it a perfect solution for both of us. I shifted round a little in my seat to face him. 'Since when?'

Alex sipped on his drink.

'Is this because of Gideon?' I asked. 'Because if it is, you needn't worry. Like I said, he's admitted he behaved badly. He doesn't know what got into him, and nor do I.'

Alex raised his eyebrows, making it clear he wasn't convinced.

'Besides, as I've also said before, it's up to me who I have living in *my* flat. No one else.'

Realising my tone was unfair, I fell quiet. Putting myself in Alex's shoes, his reluctance was understandable. Being new to the area, of course the last thing he'd want was any kind of trouble. I faced forward again. 'Look, I get it. And whether you move in or not, that's up to you.'

Alex put his glass to his lips, as if trying to hide his smile. 'You don't say.'

I knew he was teasing me and, leaning in, I gave him a playful shoulder bump. 'All I'm saying is, don't imagine problems where there aren't any. There's a room at mine if you want it. Just let me know what you decide when you're ready.' I raised my glass. 'Deal?'

Alex raised his. 'Deal.'

We both drank to seal our agreement.

'I'm sorry for turning up like this,' I said. 'The truth is, I didn't want to be on my own. Having your own place is great, until it isn't. Sometimes it gets lonely.' Realising how that might sound, I looked at Alex, mortified. 'Please don't take that the wrong way. That wasn't an attempt to pressurise you into a rental agreement.'

Alex laughed. 'I know exactly what you meant. I also live on my own remember.' He fell quiet for a moment. 'You must miss your Gran?'

I took a deep breath and exhaled. 'Always. But tonight especially.' I glanced his way. 'I really envy you.'

'Me?' Alex appeared surprised. 'Why?'

'For having a mum and a sister and a grandma who knits you scarves.'

'Don't forget my three nieces and one nephew. They'd never forgive you if you did.'

I smiled. 'That's my point. When life gets tough, you have people around to distract you. To help put things into perspective. You must be looking forward to seeing them.'

'I am.' Alex gave me a knowing look. 'But after five minutes in their company, I'll be wishing I was back here.'

I prodded Alex's arm. 'You don't mean that.'

He chuckled. 'Oh, I do.'

I still didn't believe him.

'Tell me about them,' I said.

Alex's eyes lit up. 'They're loud and messy and have absolutely zero filters. The first thing Mum'll do when I land is look me up and down and say *Have you lost weight?*'

I laughed. Whoever Alex was impersonating, it couldn't have

been his mother. There wasn't a woman on earth who sounded like that.

'Grandma will ask me when I plan on getting married, whether I have a girlfriend or not.'

'And do you?'

'Have a girlfriend?' Alex looked at me direct. 'No. I don't.'

I felt my cheeks redden. 'And Avery?' My voice cracked. 'What will she do?'

'Avery will stand there while her out of control brood charge and tackle me to the ground.'

Easily picturing the scene, I sighed, wistful. 'Sounds perfect.' Back to sitting in silence, I wondered what life would've been like if it hadn't been just me and Gran. I wondered if I'd be lucky enough to one day grow a big family of my own.

'You know what we need?' Alex suddenly asked.

I indicated my almost empty glass. 'Another drink?'

He got down from his seat and, pulling his mobile out of his pocket, grinned. 'Music.'

'You're kidding me?'

He tapped his phone screen and as Wizard's 'I Wish it Could be Christmas Every Day' began to play, he ramped up the volume. Laying his phone down on the bar, Alex held out his hand for me to take.

'You're asking me to dance?'

'I am.' He swung his hips to and fro in time with the beat. 'Come on.' He winked at me. 'You know you want to.'

Watching his shoulders sway back and forth, I laughed, unable to remember the last time I'd given myself up to gay abandon.

I recalled how on Sunday mornings Gran would turn up the radio to sing and dance her heart out while she prepared lunch. She was tone deaf and sounded like out-of-tune trombone, but she didn't care; she was having fun. As Alex continued to entice me, I heard Gran's voice telling me to go ahead; after the evening I'd had, I deserved to let loose.

I jumped down onto my feet and taking Gran's advice, accepted Alex's hand. Losing myself in the moment, all my stresses and strains dissipated. The two of us danced to one Christmas tune after another. Not only could Alex move, unlike me who'd inherited Gran's somewhat unique tone and tenor, he could sing. His vocal range was impressive.

The tempo changed as the introduction to Alexandra Burke's 'Hallelujah' kicked in. Alex's gaze met mine and as we both fell quiet, a seriousness descended. As Alex stepped towards me, I knew I should look away, crack a joke, go and sit down... anything to break the spell. But I did nothing.

Alex took my hand and clasping it, he pulled me close. I felt his other palm on the small of my back and letting him guide me, we gently swayed from side to side. Breathing in his scent of sandalwood and spices, my chest felt light and, lifting my gaze, Alex stared back at me with an intenseness I'd never experienced before. As the final song of his playlist, it came to end, but as if in a trance we carried on dancing.

The bubble that surrounded us suddenly burst, and coming back to my senses, I quickly let go of Alex and took a step back. 'I'm sorry.' I grabbed my coat and bag. 'I should go.' Running to the door, I slid open its bolt and without looking back, rushed out into the darkness.

CHAPTER 19

*A*s I sat at the till awaiting my next customer, I needed something to kick start me into picking up my needles. Page after page, I flicked through a pattern book hoping inspiration would strike. I slapped it shut. Nothing grabbed my attention.

I opened the paper bag that had lain untouched on the counter since lunch. Made with the freshest ingredients, it seemed even The Beanery's mushroom, mozzarella and pesto sandwich couldn't lift my spirits. I grimaced, discarding it again. With zero appetite, I wondered why I'd bought it in the first place. My mind and body were clearly reeling from the emotional roller coaster I'd been on.

I let out a loud frustrated growl. Christmas was fast approaching. I should have been looking forward to cosying up with Gideon in front of the fire, eating my body weight in chocolate and stocking up on tissues ready for when Alan Rickman does the dirty on Emma Thompson. Instead, I was having to wrap my head around marriage proposals, hospital dashes, reruns of Gran's death, and a clandestine dance with Alex. I cringed... especially the dance with Alex.

121

I recalled the feel of his hand in mine, the gentle pressure on my lower back, and rhythm of Alex's heart as I rested my head against his chest. Like magic, he'd drawn me into his gaze to the point I was transfixed. No man had ever looked at me with such fervour. Not even Gideon when hours earlier, he'd been about to propose. Alex both scared and excited me, when what I needed was to feel safe.

Safe? Where's the fun in that? Gran asked.

Refusing to answer her, I shook my mind free. Knowing I'd have to confront everything and everyone at some point, I was determined to delay the inevitable for as long as possible.

Picking up my phone, I checked the screen, wondering if I should message Joyce for an update on Richard. The last I'd heard he was waiting for more test results. Reassuring myself with the adage *no news is good news,* I put my phone back down. The last thing my friend needed was me bothering her; she'd be in touch when she was ready.

I frowned. As would Gideon. Having had no contact from him since he'd dropped me at the hospital, I wondered what he was playing at. For all he knew I could've been helping Joyce plan a funeral.

No matter how hard I tried to understand, the same question kept popping up in my mind. *Why would Gideon not be there for the woman he wanted to marry?*

An image of Alex guiding me to a seat at the bar intruded my thoughts. I sighed. *Why would a man who hardly knew me ensure he was?*

The shop bell signalled a welcome interruption, and I looked up to see George Farrington Senior make his entrance. Taking in his oil-stained overalls, my smile froze as I spotted the brown envelope in his hand. Dreading the invoice it no doubt contained, was one thing. The thought of getting a massive bill with no van to show for it was something else. I wrinkled my nose in anticipation. 'Did you manage to fix her?'

George tottered towards me. With his years obviously taking their toll, it was a miracle he could still get himself in and out from under the vehicles in his workshop. He rummaged in his pockets for Beryl's keys, grinning as he held them up for me to take. 'She's as good as new.'

Relief swept over me. Although picturing Beryl's numerous rust spots and torn interior, we both knew his claim was somewhat of an exaggeration. 'Thanks, George. Being without Beryl has been like having no legs.' I didn't have a clue what I'd have done if George hadn't been able to work his mechanical magic. No way could I have afforded to replace her.

'She's also had a full service so I shouldn't be seeing her for a while.'

Were George not in his work clothes, I'd have hugged him.

'She's parked up on the street outside the garage. Collect her when you're ready. As for this...' He placed the envelope down on the counter. 'There's no rush. Any time in January suits me.'

In addition to a hug, I could have kissed him.

The shop bell rang again, and my eyes widened in surprise. The last person I expected to see was Joyce. 'What are you doing here?' I raced from behind the counter and threw my arms around her. 'Please tell me it's good news.'

'Time for me to go, I see.' Making his exit, George paused. 'Glad to hear Richard's still with us,' he said to Joyce. 'A bit of a close call there, by all accounts.'

'You can say that again,' she replied. 'I'll pass on your best wishes.'

He placed a hand on Joyce's arm. 'Please do.'

Joyce waited until the door had closed behind George before speaking. 'I can't believe that man's still working. I wonder what his secret is? He's got to be well into his eighties.'

'Maybe he loves his job?'

'Or maybe he doesn't trust his son to run his business properly?' She dipped her chin as if in the know.

'If they're not already, people will be talking about you soon,' I said, turning the tables on her tittle-tattle. 'They'll be wondering why you're not at the hospital tending to your sick husband.'

'I'm not at the hospital because Richard has been discharged.' Joyce stood tall. 'He's back home thumbing the pages of his cookbooks as we speak.'

I breathed a sigh of relief.

'His follow-up blood tests and electro-whatever-gram show everything's back to normal.'

'That is good news.'

'He's a bit tired thanks to all the excitement, of course. But the doctor assures us there's nothing to worry about moving forward.'

'Well, tell him from me there's to be no more foraging.' I retook my position behind the till.

Joyce laughed. 'I think he's learnt his lesson.' Her gaze fell on my Beanery sandwich bag. 'Do you plan on eating that? Or is it just for decoration?'

I slid it towards her. 'When you say "back to normal", does that include being back...'

'In the kitchen?' Joyce nodded. 'Unfortunately.' The shop doorbell rang as she tucked in.

'What are you doing here?' Erin called out. Someone else I didn't expect to see that day, she hastened forward and threw her arms around Joyce.

'Shouldn't you be at work?' Joyce asked.

'Shouldn't you be at the hospital?' Erin replied.

'You can relax,' I said. 'Richard's home, safe and sound.'

'Thank goodness.' Erin dumped her bag on the counter. 'I

don't think I could cope with any more excitement. I've just been to see Mum. She's only gone and bought herself a smartphone. Thanks to the lad next door, I might add, who, no doubt, put the idea into her head. Those two are developing quite a friendship.' She filled her cheeks with air and slowly exhaled. 'She hasn't stopped ringing and texting, no matter how many times I tell her I'm in a meeting or with a client.' Erin shook her head. 'I feel awful spoiling her fun. But after one too many memes, I had no choice but to go round and give her the hard word.'

'How did she take it?' I asked.

'All right, I think. I've left her with Duolingo for company. Since digging out those letters, she's decided to brush up on her long-forgotten French.' Erin took another deep breath as if centring herself. 'That's enough about me and my problems.' She turned to Joyce. 'How's poor Richard really doing?'

Mid-mouthful, Joyce swallowed. 'Like I said, he's back to normal. Aside of a bit of tiredness, you'd think the other night never happened.'

Erin indicated Joyce's between-meal snack. 'That alone tells me all I need to know.'

'Yes, well, that's why I'm here. Catching you both at the same time has saved me a job.'

Erin and I looked to each other, curious.

'Richard wants to say thank you for coming to the hospital the other night. For being there. As do I, because honestly, you two, I don't think I'd have got through it on my own.'

'Like I said, that's what friends are for,' Erin said.

'You mean sisters,' I said, with a smile.

'It was so hard seeing him like that,' Joyce carried on. 'And the guilt... When I think about all the things I said about murdering him.' She delved in her handbag for a tissue. 'I'm surprised you weren't tempted to ring the police.' She wiped her hands of pesto and mozzarella. 'Anyway, by way of a thank you, Richard would like to invite you to dinner.'

As she looked from Erin to me and back again, clearly awaiting our response, we took a moment to let her words sink in.

'Gideon too. Considering we ruined your date night, Hattie.'

'That's very kind of Richard,' Erin finally said.

'Very kind,' I said.

'I know what you're thinking. That after all my complaints about his food I'm putting you both in a bit of a predicament.' Joyce tilted her head. 'But accepting his invitation would mean a lot to Richard. And to me.'

Erin and I stared back at her, neither of us knowing quite how to respond.

'The thing is,' Erin said, clearly thinking on her feet. 'I do have a lot of work on at the moment. Did I tell you about the office restructure?'

'And I've got so much to do around here.'

Joyce followed my gaze around the customer free shop.

'You know what December's like,' I said. 'A stampede can happen at a moment's notice.'

'Nice try.' Joyce looked from me to Erin. 'Both of you. But I'm not taking no for an answer.'

'A minute ago, she called us friends,' Erin said.

As I stood chuckling, the shop bell rang for a third time and looking to see who had arrived, my laughter immediately stopped.

Alex paused in the doorway, evidently surprised to see Erin and Joyce present. His eyes met mine, but neither of us spoke.

Erin looked from me to him and sensing something afoot, she turned to Joyce. 'Come on. Time for us to go.'

Joyce appeared bemused. 'Where to?'

Erin glared at Joyce, willing her to get the message, but

telepathy clearly wasn't in either woman's skill set. Erin leaned in and lowered her voice. 'Anywhere that isn't here.'

Joyce now looked from me to Alex. 'I see.' Her apparent confusion, however, showed that she didn't. She picked up her bag and turned to me. 'I'll tell Richard it's a yes then, shall I?' As Erin steered her towards the door, Joyce did her best to resist. 'What have I missed?'

Erin shovelled her out onto the street.

CHAPTER 20

lex continued to hover in the doorway. We stood silent, staring at each other. Even with the distance between us the tension was palpable.

I swallowed hard. After running out on him the way I had, I was aware I'd have to explain myself at some point. I just hadn't expected to be doing that so soon.

'I wasn't interrupting anything, was I?' Alex asked, at last, finding his voice.

Forced to compose myself, the room suddenly felt warm. 'No,' I replied, a little too quickly.

Alex took a step forward.

'Erin happened to be passing, and Joyce popped in with a dinner invite.' I waved my hands around as I spoke. 'Although I'm not sure I want to go. Apparently Richard is a terrible cook.' I let out a nervous laugh. 'Then again, you know what Joyce can be like. Or maybe you don't because you've only just moved here. Safe to say, she could be exaggerating.'

Alex smiled, making me aware my mouth was running away with itself once more. I clamped it shut and wondered what was wrong with me. Why, whenever I was within metres of Alex, did I have to rattle on?

Alex stepped forward again. 'I wanted to say I'm sorry. For my behaviour the other night.'

His apology came as a surprise, and I stepped forward too. 'No. I was the one in the wrong.' I wiped my palms down my sides. 'I'd had a tough evening. My head was all over the place and I was way too emotional.' I looked at him direct. 'I shouldn't have fled the way I did. You didn't deserve that. It was unwarranted.'

Holding my gaze, Alex came a bit closer. 'I should've been more sensitive.'

'Not at all. You were...' I recalled his hand moving up and down my back. '...great.' Yet again, Alex's presence seemed to render me powerless and like he was some sort of magnet, I moved closer still.

He closed the gap between us completely. 'The music was unnecessary.'

I envisaged us on our imaginary dance floor, twisting and twirling and singing our hearts out. I couldn't think of a better way to have rid myself of the emotional turmoil I'd experienced, and I smiled just thinking about it. 'Actually, that was the most fun I've had in ages.'

'Even so. I wouldn't want you to think I was taking advantage.'

My expression turned serious. No one could deny Alex was the epitome of tall dark and handsome, but behind his deep chestnut eyes there was a vulnerability; a need, almost, for me to believe his intentions that evening had been honourable. The fact he had the courage to show me what was going on under his surface made him even more attractive. 'I just...'

Close enough for me to smell his now familiar scent, I had to stop myself from reaching up and touching his face and as my hand brushed against his, I tingled at his touch. Our eye contact remained firm and the fluttering in my chest increased. I became aware of my own heartbeat and felt the rise and fall of my chest as desire ran through my veins.

'You just what?' Alex asked, his voice quiet and gentle.

His face slowly moved towards mine and as his lips grew closer, I wanted nothing more than to feel his kiss. My heart beat even faster as his hand rested on my waist and my breath caught as he eased my body towards him. I closed my eyes in anticipation, desperate to feel his mouth pressed against mine. My lips parted and sensing they were about to connect with his, my whole body yearned.

My mobile sounded and our eyes snapped open.

We both froze and staring at each other, didn't dare move. Finally, the phone went silent, and we immediately let go of each other. Alex ran a hand through his hair, seemingly as embarrassed as I was.

In need of a diversion, I turned to check my phone screen and seeing a missed a call from Gideon, a knot twisted in my stomach. After all my complaints about him and Julia, I felt an absolute hypocrite. I closed my eyes and scolded myself. *What was I thinking?*

Swallowing my guilt, I plastered a smile on my face and determined to pretend the last few minutes hadn't happened, spun round to face Alex. 'So, can I interest you in more wool for Grandma?'

Alex opened his mouth to speak, but no words came out.

I gestured to our surroundings. 'We've got some lovely ranges to choose from.'

Confusion flitted across his face. 'I think I'm good thanks.' He started to say something else, but evidently changing his mind Alex instead took a step backwards. He indicated the door. 'I should go.'

I fast nodded my head. 'Hmm-hmm.'

Alex moved nearer to the exit. 'I'll see you in the pub, yeah?'

Again, I nodded. 'Hmm-hmm.'

I kept my eyes on Alex as he grabbed the door handle and while a part of me wished he'd just leave already, another part wanted him to stay. I held my breath as he gave me one last look and let himself out.

I waited until he was out of sight to, at last, exhale. Racing to the door, I flipped the shop sign to closed, and turning, leant my back against the glass. Sliding downwards until my bum hit the ground, I rested my elbows on my knees. Cringing at my behaviour, I couldn't believe I'd made a fool of myself again. I closed my eyes and let my head drop into my hands.

CHAPTER 21

George Farrington hadn't been lying when he said Beryl was as good as new. Gone was her coughing and spluttering. Her engine didn't have as much as a tickle on the thirty-minute drive to Copington. Upon my arrival, I'd circled the car park three times to find a space and not once had Beryl backfired. She performed brilliantly.

I wasn't surprised to find the area crammed with vehicles. Copington was host to one of the county's best Christmas markets. An ancient town, full of winding cobbled streets and quaint historic architecture, for one week every December it was transformed into a festive shopping winter wonderland. It was the ideal place to pick up gifts for loved ones, which under the circumstances was a good job. With everything that had been going on, I'd continued to let my Christmas preparations slide and now I was really playing catch-up. Climbing out of my van and heading down the street, I was on a mission.

Thankfully, I didn't have many people to buy for. There was Erin, Joyce, and Richard... An image of Alex popped into my head, but feeling a stab of guilt, I immediately dismissed it. No way was I buying him a present. One, because I didn't want to send him another mixed message; there'd been enough of those already. And two, because abstaining gave me more cash towards a gift for Gideon. I knew getting Gideon something extra special wouldn't completely assuage the remorse I felt, but I needed to do something to make up for my actions.

Copington Christmas Market was always marked in Gran's calendar. Every year she'd shut up shop and we'd head over to delight in the sights and smells of all things festive. We'd sample food, drink hot chocolate, and treat ourselves to a hand-blown glass tree decoration or intricately iced gingerbread house. Like festive sponges, we'd soak up the atmosphere and taking it home with us, our countdown to Christmas would begin in earnest.

When Gran died, I vowed never to keep our Copington tradition again. Without her, it simply wouldn't have been the same. I hadn't planned on attending that evening either. I'd simply wanted to escape the flat and be alone with my thoughts. Jumping into my van, with no clue as to where I was going, I'd suddenly felt drawn to the market. It was as if Gran had been guiding me.

Walking along, I picked up my pace, ready to join the Christmas throng and turning one last corner, my heart danced. As soon as I saw the huge Christmas tree and familiar rows of red and white tented stalls, I immediately felt comforted. Tears threatened my eyes, and I looked up at the night sky, thanking Gran for giving me the push I needed.

Fairy lights everywhere, the whole market sparkled. Aromas from rich spices to roasted chestnuts to fried onions filled the air. Carols played through loudspeakers and children giggled as they went round and round on the festive carousel, while others struggled to contain their excitement as they waited in line to see Santa in his grotto.

Perusing the goods on offer, I saw handmade soaps and

wooden toys. Artisans like silversmiths, ceramicists and leather smiths sold their handcrafted wares. Handing over my money, I couldn't resist a zipped leather pouch for Erin. She was forever searching the bottom of her bag for something or other, and it was just the right size to hold one of her elusive lipsticks, numerous hair pins or a handful of coins.

Continuing on my way, I spotted a stall displaying woollen socks and shoes and with my curiosity piqued, I headed over for a closer look. I smiled at the vendor who sat cocooned in a thick padded coat and wore fingerless gloves. I couldn't help but admire her. Busy knitting, she worked her needles at an impressive speed. I picked up two pairs of felted slippers, one in navy and one in beige, and sitting them side by side, admired the skill with which they'd been made.

Seeing me home in on the details, the vendor put down her work.

'These are gorgeous,' I said, running my fingers along the stitches.

'They're knitted tighter so they can perfectly mould to your feet.'

'I can see that.' I raised an eyebrow. 'Pure wool?'

The woman nodded. 'Of course. In a pair of those, you'll never have numb toes again.'

Thinking they'd make a great *his and her* gift for Joyce and Richard, I knew I could have made them myself. But aware of how much work the vendor had put into her creations, I was happy to support a fellow wool crafter. 'I'll take them,' I said.

The woman indicated a sheet of mistletoe and eucalyptus design wrapping paper and ball of red ribbon. 'Together or separately?'

'Separate please.'

While the vendor got to work, I glanced around, smiling on as little ones dragged reluctant parents towards the sweet stands.

Couples, arm in arm, meandered from stall to stall and people sat at plastic dining sets, their hands tight around steaming glasses of mulled wine or mugs of hot chocolate.

A lone chap at one such table caught my attention and telling myself I was imagining things, I narrowed my eyes to better focus. *What's he doing here?* While Gideon's presence confused me, there was no denying it was him.

Collar up and scarf wrapped tight, his hands were stuffed into his coat pockets. He appeared miserable, although I supposed it was hardly breaking news that he'd want to be anywhere but Copington Christmas Market. Never mind during Yuletide, Gideon found shopping at any time of year irritating. He was the kind of person who bought only the essentials, and he usually got those online. When it came to clothes, if Gideon liked something he purchased it in every colour and only replaced items when they fell apart. An artisan-fuelled festive street market certainly didn't usually appeal to him.

Hoping to head over and surprise him before he saw me, I quickly dug into my bag and grabbed my bank card from my purse. Holding it out at the ready, it seemed the vendor wasn't the quickest at gift wrapping. Sellotaping the wrapping paper and picking up her scissors, she casually snipped a long piece of ribbon. Singing while she worked, she weaved it around the first of my two packages and tied it into a bow.

Watching her was painful and my impatience grew. As did my curiosity over Gideon's presence and I glanced his way again. It was hard not to feel sorry for him, such was his misery, and as I opened my mouth to call out and get his attention, the vendor interrupted me before I got the chance.

'Here you are.' She passed me the slipper parcels with one hand and held out her card reader with the other.

While I waited for the machine to bleep, I saw Gideon check his watch and look around as if waiting for someone. I frowned as I scanned the people in our vicinity. I didn't recognise anyone in line waiting for coffee, or, indeed, at the nearby stalls. I supposed his family could be down for a visit. I scowled. Something I'd have known if he'd been in touch.

My chest tightened, reminding me that Gideon keeping his distance wasn't the only problem in our relationship. Having almost kissed another man, my behaviour wasn't squeaky clean. Full of regret, I told myself there was no point wishing I could go back and change events. All I could do was make better choices moving forward.

I knew it would be just like Gideon to let his mum Serena go off browsing while he sat waiting for her to finish. I cringed as I looked down at my duffel coat. Already hearing her back-handed compliments, I wished I'd made more of an effort.

Finally, the machine accepted my payment and thanking the vendor, I headed towards my boyfriend. Swallowing my guilt, I held my head high as I walked. 'Gideon,' I said, making sure to smile.

'Hattie?' The colour drained from his face, and he jumped up from his seat. 'I didn't expect to bump into you.'

I let out a laugh. 'Evidently. You should have told me your family was down. We could have all got together.'

'My family?' He looked back at me bemused. 'What do you mean?'

'I assume that's why you're here.' I gestured to our surroundings. 'To show your mum and dad the sights. We both know Christmas markets aren't *your* thing, and I can't think who else you'd be here with.'

Putting a hand up to loosen his scarf, his Adam's apple bobbed up and down as he swallowed. 'Well actually I'm...' Spotting something over my shoulder, his words trailed off.

'The queue was too long,' a female voice said.

Instantly recognising it, my smile froze.

'So I went to the stand further down.'

I slowly turned. 'Julia,' I said, almost singing. 'How lovely.'

Carrying two mugs, her composure appeared to falter, but she just as quickly regained it. 'Hattie.' As her eyes darted from me to Gideon, I was clearly the last person she expected to see too.

While she looked me up and down, I returned the favour and took in her perfect make-up. Her hair cascaded down her shoulders from under a beanie and unlike me who carried a bag for life, she wore a cross-body satchel. For the first time I saw beyond Julia's expensive clothes and designer handbags. Sometimes fancy wrapping paper was worth more than the gift.

I looked to Gideon. 'The surprises just keep on coming tonight, don't they?' I said, making sure to keep my voice upbeat.

Panic written all over his face, Gideon stepped forward. 'Hattie, this isn't how it looks.'

As my gaze went from Julia to him, the guilty weight I'd been carrying suddenly vanished. Unlike Gideon, I'd resisted my attraction to Alex, even if it was only just. Neither were my actions premeditated, and I certainly hadn't been sneaking around behind anyone's back. 'And how does this look, Gideon?' Heat flushing through my body, I glared at him.

I recalled his unnecessary rudeness towards Alex and the remarks he'd made about who fancied the pants off who. Hypocrisy at its finest, Gideon had obviously been projecting his own behaviour in a classic case of *tell me you're having an affair, without telling me you're having an affair.*

'Honestly, I can explain.'

Remembering what Joyce had said about Gloria Chalmers and her husband, I looked forward to hearing Gideon's excuses.

'Oh, I'm sure you can,' I said. 'And it better be good.'

CHAPTER 22

'So this is what you get up to when you're supposed to be working, is it?'

Gideon frowned as he took my arm and pulled me away from Julia. 'One, I never said I was working tonight. And two, I didn't know you'd be here.'

Wriggling myself free of him, I watched Julia smooth down the back of her coat and settle herself onto a chair. She wrapped her brown suede gloved hands around one of the mugs of hot chocolate and took a sip. Looking my way, she gave me a sickly smile. I couldn't tell if she was being superior or whether her drink was too sweet.

My glare went from her to my boyfriend. 'Evidently.'

Cradling his elbow with one hand, Gideon used his other to rub his forehead. 'I can see how untoward this must seem.' He took a deep breath and calmed himself. 'But whatever you think is going on here, it most certainly isn't that.'

I couldn't believe he expected me to dismiss my own eyes. 'All the times I've sat around waiting for you. To be told you're not coming and half the time, that's at the last minute.'

The occasion that especially hurt was our supposed date night. I'd put so much effort into making delicious food, laying the most romantic dinner table and creating the perfect ambience in which to decorate the Christmas tree. I'd spent a fortune on fancy underwear that also ended up being a waste of time and money. Picturing myself sat there trying to coax him on the bedroom front, tears pricked my eyes. I'd never felt so cheap and unwanted.

'You have no idea about the humiliation you've put me through. As for this place, you know how much it means to me and now you've tainted it.' I waved a hand at him and Julia. 'With whatever this is.'

Gideon's fingers twitched as if he wanted to reach out to me, but I took a step back, ensuring he couldn't. 'And you had the nerve to suggest that me and Alex were up to no good.' Catching Gideon and Julia together might not excuse the fact that Alex and I had almost kissed, but as my anger rose, it sure as hell eased my guilt. I couldn't believe the emotional self-flagellation I'd put myself through, when all along Gideon had been having secret liaisons with a work colleague.

Gideon looked at me direct. 'No, I didn't.'

My nostrils flared. 'Yes, you did.'

'What I *actually* talked about was the way Alex looked at you.'

No way was Gideon going to make things about me. 'This.' Again, I indicated Gideon and Julia. 'Is more than a look.'

Gideon narrowed his eyes. He stared at me like he was delving into my soul. 'It seems to me there's more to you and Alex than you're letting on.'

Seeing him so smug, it was all I could do to keep myself from hissing. 'Don't you dare turn this around to make me the bad guy. I mean what am I supposed to think? For weeks now, I've been told you're too busy to go to the cinema. Too busy for Erin's party. Too busy for nights in even. You haven't given a second thought to me or to us. Then I find you here about to enjoy hot chocolate with her.' I scoffed. 'A stroll around a Christmas market isn't what anyone would call work, Gideon.'

People began to look our way, but I didn't care. Unlike Gideon, it seemed, who doled out apologetic smiles to everyone in the vicinity.

'You're right. I'm sorry.'

'Being sorry doesn't explain what's going on. It doesn't explain why you didn't think the two of *us* might enjoy being here. And it doesn't explain why you brought *Julia* instead?'

As if hearing her name, Julia put down her mug and rose. She clearly didn't like the attention we were garnering. 'I'm gonna get off now,' she said, keeping her eyes on Gideon. 'The two of you clearly have a lot to talk about.' Her expression seemed to say he'd got this, as if my position on the matter in no way counted. She placed a hand on Gideon's arm. 'We'll catch up tomorrow, yeah?'

Gideon nodded as she turned to leave, while my jaw slackened.

'Unbelievable,' I said, wondering if I really was that invisible to Julia.

Gideon watched her disappear into the crowd. He turned his attention back to me. 'Look, I invited Julia here because I needed her help.'

'With what?' I asked, wondering what he was talking about.

'Choosing a gift.'

'For who?'

Gideon sighed. 'Who do you think?' He stepped forward again. 'You're the only reason I'm here, Hattie.' He took my hands. 'You were right when you said I know how important this market is to you. That's why I came. I thought getting your Christmas present here would make it extra special.'

Gideon might have appeared sincere, but that didn't mean I believed him.

'I'm not like you. I'm rubbish at choosing gifts.'

I recalled the discounted gym membership he'd bought me the previous year. Along with his mother's *Atkins Diet for Beginners,* I'd stuck it in a drawer determined to wipe its very existence from my mind.

'I thought rather than disappoint you, Julia could stop me from getting things completely wrong.' He playfully rolled his eyes. 'Don't think I haven't noticed you haven't used last year's present.'

He appeared to wait for a response, but I didn't give him one.

He sighed. 'To be fair, of course, I didn't expect you to catch me out. You said you were never stepping foot in this place again.' His expression turned earnest. 'Do you genuinely believe if I'd known you'd changed your mind, I'd be here with someone else?'

I stared at him. 'After Richard's hospitalisation, I don't know what to think. I mean, did it cross your mind that the last time I'd stepped foot in *that* place was when Gran died? And because of that, I might have needed your support? First I don't hear from you and now this. You didn't even send me a text, let alone call.'

'What are you talking about?'

'Sorry?'

'I did call.'

'You didn't.'

'I most certainly did. You just didn't answer.'

My stomach sank as I recalled the point at which my phone had rung. I could still feel the touch of Alex's hand pressing on my waist as he pulled me close. I could see his lips moving towards mine. I blinked the image away. 'Days later,' I said.

'I thought you'd want some space. Besides, that doesn't change the fact that you didn't pick up.'

I felt myself blush. 'I was busy.'

Gideon raised his eyebrows. 'Too busy to call me back?'

I sat in silence at the kitchen table staring out of the window. Gran's favourite view, but I couldn't make anything out thanks to the evening darkness. Staring out into the pitch black, I wondered what she'd make of the mess I'd got myself into. If ever I needed Gran's advice it was then.

My phone lay in front of me and awaiting a text from Erin, I checked the screen for the umpteenth time. A part of me could have done without the evening ahead. However, desperate for a diversion, another part wished Erin would hurry up and land so I could get out of my own head.

I'd never experienced the instant attraction I'd had for Alex. I got butterflies just thinking about him. His playful personality, kindness and sense of family were wrapped up in the most handsome and enticing of packages. But I had to wonder if his allure would've been the same had I not felt neglected?

I bristled, aware that the issues between Gideon and me were going from bad to worse. It was no longer simply about a lack of attention. Thanks to his surreptitious trip to the Christmas market, whatever kind of relationship Gideon had with Julia, we'd well and truly gone into the realms of mistrust. Even if Gideon did seem to have an answer for everything.

Not that I considered myself blameless. Gideon had seen me through the worst experience of my life. He'd given me structure and a sense of calm in what had felt like chaos and how did I repay him?

Anyone would think you owed the man, Gran said. *Relationships aren't credit agreements, Hattie. There's no score to be kept. The last thing you should feel is* indebted *to Gideon.*

Gran might have had a point, but that didn't make me innocent. As far as I was concerned, in almost kissing Alex I'd crossed a line.

My phone bleeped, pulling me out of my reverie. Erin's text let me know she'd parked up and would meet me outside, so I put on my coat and bobble hat, grabbed my bag for life full of goodies and made my way down to the street.

Locking the shop door behind me, I glanced around, taking in Settledown's festive lights and window displays as I waited for Erin to arrive. Recalling the Yuletide frivolity I'd shared with Gran, I wondered if Christmas would ever feel the same again. I'd known the previous year, my first without her, was always going to be hard. But I'd navigated my way through it, all the while telling myself the following year would be easier. I sighed. That following year was upon me and it already felt wrong.

My eyes settled on The Royal Oak in the distance. I guessed Alex was behind the bar, pencil in hand, sketching the customers around him. Stood there torn and confused, I damned the brewery for its reshuffle.

'Great minds think alike,' Erin said.

I spun round to see my friend approach.

'You've brought snacks too.' She indicated her own bag of delights. 'If Richard's cooking is as bad as Joyce claims, at least we won't starve.'

I smiled as we set off towards the town square. Determined to hide my unhappiness, the last thing I wanted was to spoil everyone's evening.

'Everything okay?' Erin asked.

I evidently wasn't hiding it well enough.

I realised Erin had suddenly stopped walking and coming to a standstill with her, I could see by her raised eyebrows that my friend wanted answers. Hesitating, I wasn't sure sharing my woes was a good idea. One word in front of Joyce and my whole sorry tale would be out in the open. I'd be the subject of gossip and before I knew it, when it came to me, Gideon and Alex, the key word on the street would be *polyandrous*.

But I needed to talk to someone.

'Everything's such a mess,' I said. 'And I don't know what to do about it.'

Erin's face relaxed. 'Fancy a drink?' She gestured to The Royal Oak.

I fast shook my head.

'Okay.' She glanced around and spotting a park bench, linked her arm in mine. 'Come on.' Leading me straight to it, we sat down on the frost-covered pew. She reached into her bag, and pulling out a pack of six mince pies, ripped it open, taking out one for me and one for herself. 'Is this to do with Gideon, by any chance?' she asked, biting into hers.

I let out a dry laugh. 'And the rest.' I took a deep breath, not sure where to start. 'You know how he's been distant? Always working and not putting time aside for me.'

Continuing to eat, Erin nodded.

'Then he met Alex, and he seemed to change. Well, the other night at the restaurant, I thought he was going to propose.'

Erin immediately swallowed. 'Really?'

'I mean, I don't know for sure because he didn't get chance to finish, but it certainly sounded that way.'

'Is marriage what you want?'

'If you'd have asked me that a few weeks ago I'd have said definitely.'

'And now?'

'I don't think that matters. After Joyce rang, and it was all systems go to get to the hospital, he hasn't brought it up again.'

'Not even when he rang to check on Richard?'

'That's the other thing. He didn't even check on me.' I let out a deep, weighted sigh. 'Which makes me wonder if I'd read the restaurant situation wrong. Although I suppose in the cold light of day he could've changed his mind.'

'Maybe he panicked. Felt threatened by you renting a room to Alex, which prompted the conversation. Then he realised how daft he was being and backed off.'

'Maybe.'

'Weird he didn't contact you though. To make sure you were all right.'

I scoffed. 'It gets weirder. I saw him at Copington Christmas Market last night and he wasn't alone. He was with Julia.'

Erin straightened up in her seat. 'You're kidding me?'

'He said she was helping him choose my Christmas present.'

'Do you believe him?'

'I want to.' I twisted round slightly to face Erin. 'But it's like he's given me one doubt too many and what little trust I have left is hanging on by a thread.'

Erin handed me another mince pie.

'Unless I'm using him as a smoke screen because the problem's with me. It's not like I'm completely innocent in all of this.'

'I take it we're now talking about Alex?'

My stomach lurched. 'What makes you say that?'

'One, he fancies you.'

I rolled my eyes. She was beginning to sound like Gideon.

'And two, when you'd rather sit on a bench in the freezing cold than go in there...' Erin pointed to The Royal Oak. '...where there's a real fire and a warm drink on offer, I have to assume there's something going on between the two of you.'

'There's nothing going on. Not really.'

Erin looked at me like she knew better.

Despite wishing I hadn't, I told myself I'd started the conversation so I may as well finish. 'When you dropped me off at my flat other night, I couldn't face going in, so I called at the pub. I hadn't realised it was closing time, but Alex offered me a drink anyway.'

Erin's eyes widened. 'Just the two of you?'

I nodded.

'Now things are getting interesting.'

'Nothing happened. I was missing Gran and Alex was happy to listen. Then we danced.' I smiled, as I pictured us. I couldn't remember the last time I'd laughed like that. 'Then this slow number came on and...' I fell quiet.

'And what?' Erin didn't even try to hide her eagerness.

'And nothing.'

Erin appeared confused.

'I realised what I was doing, and I ran out the door.'

Erin seemed to deflate. Brow suddenly knitted, she stared at me. 'So let me get his straight. You're feeling bad over something you *didn't* do?'

'Alex came by the shop the next day to apologise.'

Erin's bemusement continued. 'For what?'

'That's what I thought. He doesn't have a responsibility to Gideon. I do. Which is why I should've stopped Alex when he put his arms around me.'

'So the two of you did kiss?'

'No. But the only reason we didn't was because my phone rang.'

Erin looked at me like I'd gone mad. 'So if you still didn't kiss, what's the problem?'

'The problem is, I wanted to. More than anything.'

'I'd like to kiss Alex, but I'm not losing sleep over the fact that I haven't.'

'But you're not in a relationship. You're not acting like there's one rule for Gideon and another for yourself.' I sighed. 'I feel like such hypocrite.'

'So what are you going to do?'

I wrinkled my nose. 'I wish I knew.'

'Let me put it this way, if Gideon wasn't on the scene, could you see you and Alex getting together? As a couple.'

Frowning, that was a question I refused to think about, let alone answer.

'Okay. Then can you imagine yourself still with Gideon in years to come? Marriage, kids, the lot.'

'I used to. When Gran passed away, I felt so alone. Gideon saved me. If I hadn't met him, I doubt I'd have my sanity, let alone the shop. That's what makes this situation so hard. Back then he was patient and understanding. Everything I needed.'

'And now?'

I shrugged.

Erin looked at me, her expression heartfelt. 'Not all relationships are meant to last, Hattie. Some are meant to come and go. Of course, whether or not that includes yours with Gideon, only you can decide. Either way, just know you're not beholden to him.' Erin put a hand on mine. 'Although, if you want my advice...'

Thinking back to the fancy underwear situation, I wasn't sure I did.

'When you don't know what to do, don't do anything.'

I supposed that made sense. I wasn't exactly in the right frame of mind to be making serious decisions. 'The fact that it's

Christmas isn't helping. I was hoping for a bit of holiday fun. Instead, I'm wondering if I'll be like Macaulay Culkin's Kevin McAllister, spending it home alone.'

'If the worst comes to the worst, you can always celebrate with me and Mum.'

I chuckled. 'Thank you. The way things are going, I might have to take you up on that.' Ready to talk about something else, I bit into my mince pie. 'Should we really be eating these?'

'After what we've heard about Richard's cooking, most definitely.'

My phone bleeped, letting me know a text had come through.

'That'll be Joyce,' Erin said. 'She's probably wondering where we've got to.'

Checking the screen, I frowned. 'Now there's a surprise.'

'Don't tell me it's Gideon.'

I nodded.

'He's not bowing out, is he?'

'Not quite. But he is going to be late.'

'Brave man,' Erin said. 'After being caught out and about with another woman you'd think he'd be trying to impress.'

I shook my head at his audacity. 'Exactly.'

CHAPTER 24

Settledown was small and compact, so it didn't take Erin and me long to reach the edge of town where Joyce lived. Talking to Erin might not have solved my problems, but it had lifted my mood and as we turned one last corner to walk down Joyce's street, I felt a lot more relaxed.

'I've always liked these properties,' I said, admiring the row of immaculate cottages.

'In all my time in real estate,' Erin said. 'I don't remember seeing any of these advertised on the open market. It's all word of mouth. As soon as there's a whiff of one coming up for sale, it's snapped up. That's how sought-after they are.'

Each with their own long front garden, every house embodied the Christmas spirit. Some were festooned in brightly lit decorations that had to render them visible from space. Blow up Santas, acrylic snowmen and numerous red-nosed Rudolphs contrasted with more aesthetically stylish giant-antlered reindeer in woven rattan. Holly wreaths were pinned to almost all their doors and bauble-clad trees sat in windows.

Joyce's cottage, with its solar lanterns, festive hanging baskets and boxwood globes fitted in perfectly.

'I wonder what delights are on tonight's menu,' Erin said, as we reached Joyce's garden gate.

After what we'd heard, I dreaded to think. 'I guess we're about to find out.'

We made our way to the cottage door and knocked.

'Come on in,' Richard called out.

Not knowing what to expect, Erin and I looked to each other in anticipation. We took a moment to prepare ourselves and nodding to signal our readiness, made our entrance.

'Jesus.' Erin immediately gripped the door frame.

We should have known no amount of mental priming could prepare us. The attack on our nostrils was instant.

I grimaced at the smell. Perhaps Gideon had had the right idea in working late, and I felt tempted to ring him and ask if he needed an assistant.

As Erin and I took off our hats and coats to hang on the bottom of the banister, Richard appeared in the hall from the kitchen. Failing to notice our discomfort, he had a tea towel slung over his shoulder and a wooden spoon in his hand. 'Good timing,' he said. 'Dinner's almost ready.'

Struggling to ignore the unfortunate aroma, Erin and I forced ourselves to smile.

I tried to hold my breath and speak at the same time. 'Can't wait,' I said, my voice croaking. 'It's good to see you looking so well after your foraging mishap.'

'Don't worry. There are no horse chestnuts on tonight's menu.' Richard puffed out his chest. 'We're on spaghetti bolognaise.'

Appreciating the clarification, my nose tried and failed to uncover any hint of garlic and basil. 'Yummy,' I replied.

Richard delighted in what wasn't really a compliment and seeing his sheer joy, I understood why Joyce hadn't the heart to be honest with him.

'I wouldn't call it any old spaghetti bolognaise, mind,' Richard continued.

'Me neither,' Erin said.

'Gordon Ramsey and Delia Smith have nothing on me.'

I heard myself wince. This from a man with no training, no experience, and no palate.

'You got that right,' Erin said.

'The trick is to introduce an array of secret ingredients. Not just one or two.'

While my eyes began to water, Richard's widened, as if waiting for us to hazard a guess at what his secret ingredients were. 'I'll make it easy for you. You're only looking for four.'

Erin and I made a show sniffing the air. With nothing discernible coming through, we were in danger of being there all night.

'It's best if you keep things like that to yourself,' I said.

Richard appeared crestfallen.

'Otherwise, people will steal your ideas.'

'No, they won't,' Erin muttered under her breath.

'I take your point.' Richard cocked his head. 'We seem to be a guest short. No Gideon tonight?'

'He's been delayed,' Erin replied. She gave me a furtive look. 'Something came up at work.' Like me, she was clearly envious of that fact.

Richard scoffed. 'What? Again?'

'Busy time of year,' I said, toeing Gideon's party line.

Richard raised his wooden spoon. 'No problem. I'm happy to save him a plate.'

I envisaged Gideon sat at his laptop, rubbing his eyes thanks to its glaring screen and a mountain of complicated paperwork. He probably hadn't eaten since lunch and, knowing him, that would've consisted of a soggy plastic-wrapped sandwich and a bag of crisps. As I wondered if I should forewarn him and suggest he pick something up before landing, a picture of Julia, with her big brown eyes and cascading raven waves also popped into my head. 'Please do.' I gave Richard the most honest smile I'd given him since arriving. 'And make it a big one.'

As Richard turned back to the kitchen, Erin shook her head at my naughtiness.

'Gideon needs to realise there's more to life than work,' Richard called out as he disappeared.

I couldn't help but let out a laugh. 'It's not that long ago you were just as bad.'

Richard popped his head back through the doorway. 'And don't I know it.'

Erin and I headed to the lounge in search of Joyce.

'At last! First I thought you weren't coming, then you stand chatting in the hallway.' Joyce eyed our bags. 'Can't you see I'm wasting away?' She waved her hands down the front of her fuller figure. 'And look at my cheekbones.' She thrust her face forward. 'I'm skeletal.'

'I'm surprised you're still alive,' Erin said. 'I know you told us Richard's cooking was bad. But whatever's on that stove it most certainly isn't spaghetti bolognaise.' She paused. 'He did check his sell-by dates, didn't he? Because when it goes off, beef can be rancid.'

'I'm sorry, but I did my best.' Joyce put a hand up. 'I tried to intervene but as is now customary, he wouldn't let me anywhere near the cooker. Anyway, enough of that. Please tell me you brought food?'

Erin indicated her stash and without warning, Joyce made a grab for it. She pulled out the opened box of mince pies. 'Thank goodness.' She clutched the festive treats to her chest. 'Richard hasn't left the house all day so I'm famished.' Eager to sample its wares, Joyce shoved her hand inside the cardboard. Training her eyes on me and Erin, she froze, and her smile vanished. 'How could you?' Her fingers wiggled inside the packaging and, producing one solitary mince pie, she double-checked the inside of the box. She returned her attention back to us. 'Do you want me to die from starvation?'

I indicated my bag for life. 'Don't worry. There's more in here.'

'You'd think he'd learned his lesson after the foraging,' Joyce said. 'And realise that he's no Alain Ducasse. But he's getting worse. If another new kitchen gadget enters this house, I won't be responsible for what happens.' She released a drawn-out sigh. 'Maybe that's the answer. Maybe I have no choice *but* to take action.'

'What do you mean?' I asked.

Joyce stuffed the single mince pie into her mouth whole. Investigating the other foodstuffs on offer, she suddenly thrust the bag behind her back. As Richard appeared in the doorway, her cheeks bulged. She immediately stopped chewing and attempted a smile.

'Dinner is served,' Richard said.

While her husband led the way to the dining room, Joyce nudged Erin and me forward.

'I'm not sure I can do this,' Erin said.

'Me neither,' I said.

'Follow my lead,' Joyce said, frantically trying to swallow. 'And you'll be okay.'

Sharing a look, Erin and I both doubted that.

Joyce finally rid her mouth of food. 'Trust me. I'm an expert.'

CHAPTER 25

I'd often wondered how actors managed to look like they were eating when they weren't. Thanks to Joyce's masterclass, I finally had the answer. Worthy of her own Oscar, the woman's sleight of hand was impressive.

I watched her cut into her pasta and push it around her plate, manipulating it in such a way that her portion appeared to shrink. She put her fork to her mouth numerous times, but on close inspection her food never really touched her lips, let alone made it into her belly.

Following Joyce's suggestion, both Erin and I did our best to follow her lead, but neither of us had anywhere near as much success.

Unable to take any more, I put my knife and fork down. Filling my cheeks with air, I exhaled pretending I was full. 'I couldn't eat another morsel,' I said.

Erin threw herself back in her seat. 'Same here.'

I took in Richard's confident expectation as he looked to each of us. It seemed the awkwardness around the table was palpable to all but him.

He rubbed his hands together. 'So, what did you think?'

Joyce put her palms up, withdrawing herself from the discussion. 'You already know what an admirable job I think you're doing.'

As Richard's gaze fell on me, I shifted in my seat. The last thing I wanted to do was hurt him. I picked up my glass of wine and taking a huge gulp, hoped it would help me swallow the ball of minced beef that had stuck in my gullet. 'Your cooking ability has certainly come as a surprise.' I picked up a napkin and wiped my mouth.

Chin held high, Richard looked to Joyce with a satisfied smile. 'Did you hear that, love?'

I pushed my plate away. 'I've never tasted a bolognaise like it.'

'It certainly has some interesting flavours,' Erin said.

Richard beamed. 'That'll be the secret ingredients I mentioned.'

'I'm only sorry I couldn't finish.'

Richard's eyes lit up. 'Then why don't I do you a doggy bag?'

'No!' As Richard's joy vanished, Erin realised the sharpness of her tone. She composed herself. 'I'm sorry, Richard. It's just that I've got this embarrassing medical condition.' She put a hand up to her chest and in typical Erin-style, spoke with such confidence. 'It's rare, so you might not have heard of it. But I suffer from Oompa-loompa-ti-itis.'

While I raised my eyebrows, convinced there was no way Richard would fall for that, Joyce let out a loud snigger. Immediately correcting it with a coughing fit, she picked up her glass of wine and taking a drink, tapped her chest to further disguise her amusement.

'And while tonight's menu has been a bit of a treat,' Erin continued. 'If I eat too much pasta... Well, you of all people know the dangers of eating the wrong foods.'

Richard opened his mouth to speak but Erin interrupted him.

'Don't worry,' she said. 'It's not life threatening. I just turn orange. It's like jaundice, you see. But without the yellow.'

As we all stared at Erin, dumbfounded, the doorbell rang signalling Gideon's arrival.

CHAPTER 26

My stomach grumbled as I stood at the hob stirring the soup I'd opened for dinner. But while my body wanted something more substantial, with Gideon's digestive system still recovering from Richard's spaghetti bolognaise and me having not long shut up the shop, I had neither the time nor the inclination to cook up two different dishes.

My chest felt light, as if warning me something was about to happen. To calm my anxiety, I watched the spoon go round and round, all the while breathing in tandem with the circular motion. I checked the clock. It wouldn't be long before Gideon landed, and I wondered what he'd have to say for himself.

Gideon and I hadn't properly talked since meeting at Copington Christmas Market. After he'd explained Julia's presence, we'd wandered around the stalls for a time. However, unlike the couples around us who'd kept each other close, we remained feet apart. Our conversation had been polite, but we were both as uncomfortable as each other. Me, because I wasn't sure I believed his reason for being there. Gideon, because he wasn't sure I believed him either.

He'd walked me back to the car park, and I hadn't seen him since, apart from at Richard's thank-you dinner, which wasn't exactly heart-to-heart conducive.

Having missed the opportunity to learn from Joyce's food vanishing masterclass, Gideon proved himself a real trooper. When it came to clearing his huge plate of food, forkful after forkful went into his mouth and all under Richard's watchful eye. It was a spaghetti bolognaise that none of us would ever forget, and Erin, Joyce and I couldn't help but admire Gideon's stoicism. I still hadn't figured out Richard's secret ingredients. Thanks to Gideon's subsequent tummy issues, I considered this a blessing.

I'd done a lot of thinking since then; questioning recent events until my brain hurt. But with no proof to say Gideon was up to no good, or, indeed, that he wasn't, I'd taken Erin's advice about not making any decisions until I knew which course of action was right. Much to my surprise, Gideon had clearly been reflecting too, and I was relieved when he phoned to say we needed to talk, and that he was coming round.

I recalled his tone. Serious and to the point, I wondered if he was about to call off our relationship. Thanks to the way things were between us, I wouldn't have blamed him. I'd thought about doing the same thing. 'Unless...' Suddenly panicked, I remembered his last attempt at a heart-to-heart. Dismissing my fears, I told myself I was being daft. *No way is Gideon about to get down on one knee.* I chewed on my lip. *Is he?*

As I tried to picture what married life with Gideon might look like, an image of Alex appeared my head. A man who made my heart race and mouth spout drivel every time I was near him. Who smelled delicious and made my body tingle from the most innocent of touches. A guy who saw me in a way no other man had before. Being around Alex was thrilling. He tempted me to cross boundaries I'd never dreamed of crossing. He wasn't safe or staid like Gideon.

To hell with safe and staid, Gran said.

I looked up to the heavens. 'Easy for you to say.' I frowned, as I pictured Alex the night of that office Christmas party. Throwing his cocktail shaker in the air, he appeared to revel in the female attention he received. I sighed. 'Men like him don't just turn women's heads, Gran, they break hearts.'

Alex isn't like that. He's different.

I rolled my eyes, aware that she couldn't know that. 'Gideon helped me through my grief.'

If he's such a support, where was he the other night after the hospital? Gran asked. *And what about Julia? Is he helping her too?*

Done talking about it, I turned off the hob.

Hearing footsteps on the stairs, I checked the time again. I'd left the back door open for him, so it had to be Gideon on his way up. I steeled myself in readiness of our much-needed conversation.

'Something smells good,' he said, as he entered.

I considered the empty soup tin in the bin, knowing Gideon wouldn't be quite so complimentary if he saw it. 'Just in time,' I said, indicating the pan.

Gideon took off his jacket and hung it on the back of a dining chair. He loosened his tie and while I grabbed a serving ladle, he reached into the cupboard for a couple of bowls.

'Nice to know your tummy's almost better,' I said.

Gideon tapped a box that protruded from his shirt chest pocket. 'Imodium. My new best friend.'

I spooned our dinner into the bowls, and while he carried them over to the table, I got the butter from the fridge and bread from the bread bin.

'Busy day?' Gideon asked as we took our seats.

'Very,' I replied. 'You?'

'The same.'

Our continued politeness was both understandable and uncomfortable.

My hand tightened around my spoon. I wanted Gideon to tell me about some exchange he'd had with a client or some difficult accounting arithmetic he'd had to tackle. I wanted to tell him about the customers who'd visited the shop and talk about my latest wool craft project. Instead, we both ate in silence. As the air grew thick with tension, I struggled to swallow, and my appetite waned, so I put my spoon down altogether. It was a quiet I didn't know how to break.

Finally, Gideon finished eating and pushed his empty bowl to one side. Resting his arms on the table, he regarded me. 'I've been thinking.'

My pulse quickened. The last time Gideon had spoken like that he'd been about to propose. Hoping he wasn't about to try again, I rose and gathering items off the table, carried them over to the sink. 'What about?' I closed my eyes, dreading his next words. The last thing I wanted to do was hurt Gideon, but our relationship wasn't stable enough for marriage, something that deep down he had to know too.

'Christmas.'

My brain hit pause, and I spun round. I'd been so busy flitting from one extreme to the other, in a case of break-up versus marriage, I hadn't thought to consider anything in between. 'Oh.' Relief swept over me. 'Okay.'

Gideon clasped his hands. 'Well, we haven't really talked about it. Nothing's been planned.'

I took in his earnestness. Spending time together over the holidays would certainly give us the chance to work through our issues and if all went well, maybe we'd have some fun for a change. The fact that Gideon had thought along those lines made me almost giddy.

Glad to be focusing on something positive, I scrambled in a drawer for a pen and grabbing a notepad, retook my seat at the table. It felt good to know the Christmas I'd been hoping for might come to fruition and taking a deep breath, I let out a satisfied sigh. 'I suppose we should start with deciding what we want for dinner.'

Gideon wrinkled his nose and pulled on his ear.

'Don't worry. I'm not a complete idiot in the kitchen. I just need to be methodical when it comes to the prep work.' Flipping open the notepad, I wrote the word 'dinner' and underscored it. 'Plus, I've helped Gran enough times over the years to know what's involved and I'm sure you did the same with Serena.' I smiled. 'Between us we'll do a great job.'

I envisaged us both singing along to Christmas songs as we peeled, diced and sliced. 'I'm thinking carrots, parsnips, potatoes... feel free to jump in with your suggestions.' My smile tightened as I pictured a pink featherless bird sat waiting to be freed of its giblets. I looked to Gideon. 'Are you okay dealing with the turkey?'

'I was thinking about maybe spending it at my parents' house.'

I paused in my writing. That was the last thing I expected to hear. 'Why?' The previous year's festive experience wasn't one I wanted to repeat, and my heart sank at the mere prospect.

'Because it will do us good.'

Gideon looked at me as if waiting for me to respond, but staring back at him, I didn't know what to say.

'Things between us haven't been right recently and being around family might help put things into perspective.'

Despite wishing I didn't, I appreciated Gideon's reasoning. Gran being dead hadn't stopped me turning to her during difficult times and while our conversations might be a trick of the mind, talking things through helped. I fiddled with the corner of the notepad, insisting I should be pleased. Gideon viewing his parents as a source of support for both of us meant he hadn't shut me out or given up on our relationship.

But theirs was a house I couldn't fully relax in, let alone be myself. On the very few occasions I'd met Gideon's parents, even on neutral territory, I'd felt judged. They regarded me with a mix of disdain and suspicion. As if I wasn't smart or stylish enough to join their ranks. They treated me like I was some country bumpkin, not a second-generation business owner.

'No problem,' I said, pushing my worries aside.

Gideon jerked his head. 'Really? That's all you have to say?'

I shrugged. 'What else is there?'

Gideon looked at me bemused. 'I expected at least some resistance.'

'If it's important to you, then that's all there is to it.'

'Wow.' Gideon shook off his surprise. 'Thank you.'

I flipped the notebook shut and placed the discarded pen on top of it. 'Are you talking about going for just the day? Or is the plan to stay longer?'

'I think travelling up Christmas Eve would be better. As would taking the train. The last train, in fact. That way Mum and Dad can't insist I do any of the running around if they've forgotten something.'

As selfish as that sounded, I sort of agreed. Should Gideon pick up the wrong brand of cranberry sauce, knowing Serena, the blame would inevitably fall on me.

'I can make that work. I was staying open until 5pm anyway. Just make your way over here once you're done and we can go from Settledown station.'

Gideon frowned.

'Don't worry. You don't have to cut your afternoon short. Take as long as you like. I'm just thinking while you're organising your end, I can be getting my stuff together. And we'll no doubt want snacks for the journey, which I'll sort out at the same time. A few sandwiches and a bit of a salad should be enough, don't you think?'

Gideon opened his mouth to speak, but knowing from experience what was coming, I jumped in before he got the chance. 'No, Gideon, your mum can't simply throw something in the oven for us when we land. It's her Christmas Eve too and the last thing she'll want is to be stuck in the kitchen.'

'But...'

Having conceded enough already, I gave him a stern look. 'No buts. We're more than capable of feeding ourselves.'

CHAPTER 27

I was in no rush to get to The Royal Oak for our Crochet Club meet-up. But while I'd so far managed to avoid Alex since his visit to The Knitting Nook, unless I wanted to explain to Joyce why a venue change was called for, I knew I couldn't hide from him forever. Already ten minutes late, I was determined to delay the inevitable for as long as I could and sauntering along, I ignored the cold in favour of ensuring Joyce and Erin would be there upon my arrival, drinks at the ready.

Reaching the pub, I took a deep breath and pushing on the heavy door, let myself in. Scanning the room in search of my friends, my stomach sank. Erin and Joyce were nowhere to be seen.

In the middle of topping up Ted's pint, Alex looked my way, making it impossible for me to flee even though I wanted to.

Buying myself time, I headed for a table in the corner to dump my bobble hat and coat and taking them off, I scolded myself. If I hadn't complained about Gideon working too much, I wouldn't have set off the chain of events leading to the mess I'd got myself into. Rubbing my wrist, I braced myself for a hard yet necessary conversation with Alex.

As I stepped forward, the pub doors burst open, and I spun round to see a flustered Erin charge in.

'Sorry I'm late.' Clocking my presence, she hurried straight past me. 'What're you having? The usual?'

Grateful for the last-minute reprieve, I watched her plonk her bag down on the bar and unzipping it, stick her hand inside. Unable to find her purse, she groaned and tipped everything out to continue her search. Menopause, work, or both, Erin had clearly had a bad day.

I headed back to the table and sat down. Despite the clear view I had of Erin and Alex, I resisted looking over. Trying to act natural, I picked up a beer mat and instead, focused my attention on that. Hearing laughter, my resolve broke and my gaze landed on Alex just as his landed on mine. My cheeks reddened and I quickly diverted my eyes back to the piece of cardboard, which I pretended to read until a drink was placed in front of me.

'I am so ready for this,' Erin said. 'I've had the day to beat all days.' Taking her coat off she plonked herself down and drinking a huge mouthful of wine, she seemed to savour every millilitre. 'You know that restructure I mentioned?' She wiped her lips with the back of her hand. 'Well, it transpires it's more of a downsizing. And with too many staff members for the roles available, some team members have been asked to interview. For their own jobs, no less.' She bristled. 'And yes, that does include me.'

I stared at Erin, horrified on her behalf.

'Apparently, the *powers that be* have decided they need to make sure I'm still the right fit. As it's come to their attention that I might not be up to the job anymore.' Erin shook her head, her expression pinched. 'We don't need three guesses to work out where that information came from. All lies of course.' She sighed. 'When I think of all the money I've brought in over the years. That I still bring in.'

'Oh, Erin, I don't know what to say.'

'Of course, not content with a simple Q and A, they want a full-on presentation.' Picking her glass up again, Erin waved it around while she talked. 'To take place the first week in January, I might add. Which means Christmas is out the window.' Finally, she fell silent and put her drink down. She sighed and looked at me direct. 'What am I going to do, Hattie? I can't lose this job. It's all I've got.'

I reached over with a comforting hand. 'It'll be procedure. A box-ticking exercise to cover their behinds. You'll get the job.'

Erin didn't look convinced. 'Not if Callum has his way. He's been out for me from day one.' Her brow knitted. 'I suppose some people just don't like strong women.'

'You could always take over the shop next to me?' I said, trying to raise her spirits. 'Settledown could do with its own estate agent.'

'You mean start again? At my age?' Erin let out a laugh. 'Nice idea, but I don't think so.' As Erin played with the stem of her glass, her phone bleeped.

Usually one to respond straight away, I was surprised to see her ignore it.

'Don't worry. It'll be a meme from Mum.' She rolled her eyes. 'I'll, no doubt, get a few more before the evening's out.' She took another deep breath and exhaled. 'Things with her aren't exactly helping. The lad next door may as well move in, he's round there so often. But will Mum hear a word from me about that? Oh, no. For some reason she likes him.'

'Can't you speak to his dad?'

'I've tried. He never answers the door.' Erin stared down at her hands. 'She's going to hate me for it, but I've arranged to take Mum on a tour of that residential home on the way out of town.'

My eyes widened. 'Without talking to her first?'

Erin screwed up her face and nodded. 'Breaking that bit of news is something else I've got to look forward to.' She drank another mouthful of wine. 'I'm sorry to dump all this on you. Everything's just so frustrating at the moment.'

'You're not dumping anything on anyone. We're friends remember. I'm here to help. Listening is the least I can do. You keep talking.'

Erin straightened herself up. 'Nope. I'm done. It's time to move the conversation on.' She shook her woes free. 'Tell me about what you've been up to. Have you sorted things with Gideon?'

I rolled my eyes. 'Yes and no.'

Erin narrowed hers. 'Meaning?'

'Meaning I'm still none the wiser about Julia and he certainly knows nothing about what happened with Alex. But he did suggest we spend Christmas with his parents.'

'And how do you feel about that? Considering last year.'

I wrinkled my nose. 'I don't want to go, if that's what you mean.'

'Don't tell me.' Erin put a hand up. 'But you agreed anyway?' She knew me too well.

My shoulders slumped. 'It was the least I could do after you know what.' Without thinking, I glanced at the bar area to see Alex looking back at me. Both of us clearly as embarrassed as each other, he quickly picked up his pencil and I fast looked to Erin.

'You'd have to be blind not to see how much that man likes you.' Erin leaned towards me and lowered her voice. 'I mean *really* likes you. In fact, if you ask me–'

'I'm not asking you anything.'

'I know. But if you were–'

The pub door flew open, and interrupting Erin mid-sentence, Joyce raced in. Charging towards us, she wore a beaming smile.

'At least one of us is happy,' Erin said, straightening herself up.

'Sorry I'm late. But I had some news to break to Richard.'

I couldn't remember the last time I'd seen Joyce so energised and there was no denying her excitement was contagious. 'Good news, I see.'

'Do tell,' Erin said. 'I need cheering up.'

Unable to contain herself, Joyce put her coat to one side and took a seat. 'Remember me saying if Richard continued insisting he's Gordon Ramsey, I'd have to act? Well, he finally pushed me over the edge.'

I stared at Joyce, confused. After all her talk of murdering the man, I struggled to reconcile her words with her demeanour. 'And that's a good thing because...?'

Erin chuckled. 'What did he do?'

'Only the worst thing imaginable.'

With his spaghetti bolognaise still fresh in my mind, I couldn't see how he'd top that.

'He informed me he'd be making Christmas dinner.' Joyce laughed, furthering my confusion. 'Leaving me no choice but to do the only thing I could...' As if waiting for us to guess what that was, her gaze went from me to Erin.

'Pack your bags?' I asked, tentative.

'See a divorce lawyer?' Erin added.

Joyce shook her head.

'You've put him on a flight to Nial's like you suggested?'

'Even better.' Joyce clapped her hands. 'I've booked us on a cruise.' She squealed. 'A festive cruise. We leave on Christmas Eve.'

'I'm impressed,' Erin said.

Pleased for Joyce, I put a hand up to my chest. 'Me too. But how? At such short notice.'

'Sally at Elite Travel found it for me. Through one of her special contacts, of course.'

Erin tapped Joyce's arm. 'I hope you've got a couple of posh dresses. You know, for when you dine at the captain's table.'

'How does Richard feel about this?' I asked, curious.

'Unless he's prepared to lose a whole lot of money, it doesn't matter how he feels.' Joyce wiggled her shoulders in excitement. 'I waited until it was arranged and paid for before I told him.'

'A woman after my own heart,' Erin said.

'I'm so excited, you wouldn't believe. It's years since I've had a holiday.' Joyce rose to her feet. 'I think this calls for a celebration, don't you? Cocktails all round, is it?'

I'd never seen Joyce with a spring in her step before and as she headed to the bar, I couldn't help but smile. 'I'd rather a cruise than Christmas at the Mayhews,' I said.

'Think yourself lucky. At least you'll get to celebrate. Apart from watching the King's College Choir with Mum, which she insists on every year no matter what, I'll be spending mine making PowerPoint slides.'

Joyce returned to the table. 'How does a White Christmas Mojito sound? Rum, mint, lime, and coconut cream. And a couple of other things that I can't remember.'

'Delicious,' Erin said.

Joyce turned to Alex and gave him a thumbs up. 'He's going to bring them over. Oh, and I said he should join us.'

My heart skipped a beat. 'Why?'

My question appeared to bemuse Joyce. 'One, because when it comes to saying cheers, the more the merrier. Two, because it's lonely over there on his own. Three, because as your soon-to-be tenant, he's an honorary member of our Crochet Club.' Joyce shrugged. 'How many reasons do you need?'

I looked to Erin for assistance, but none was forthcoming. Instead, she picked up her wine glass and raised it.

CHAPTER 28

'Oh my word,' Joyce said as Alex placed a tray of drinks on the table. 'These are like Christmas decorations.'

She was right. Alex's White Christmas Mojitos looked too good to consume. He'd mixed rum and soda water with thick and creamy coconut milk, poured it over crushed ice and muddled mint, lime and sugar. Sat on what could only be described as a snowy mountain in a glass, pomegranate seeds served as a bright and festive garnish, giving the cocktail a delicious winter wonderland vibe.

The only seat available was the one opposite me and hesitating over taking it, Alex met my gaze. He smiled, but I could see it was forced.

'What are you waiting for?' Joyce patted the vacant spot. 'Sit down.'

Despite his reluctance, Alex did as he was told.

'Cheers, everyone,' Joyce said.

Trying to summon the expected enthusiasm, I raised my glass. 'Cheers.'

Savouring the flavours, Joyce swooned. 'This definitely tastes as good as it looks. Talk about feeding your Christmas spirit.'

'I agree,' Erin said, putting her glass down. 'Alex, you're a genius.'

His furtive glance towards the bar told me he was desperate for Ted to finish his pint so he could excuse himself. Having never seen Alex so uncomfortable, my chest ached.

'So what are you doing for Christmas, Alex?' Joyce asked.

His eyes lit up. 'I'm heading home to spend it with family.'

As he and Joyce shared their expectations of the upcoming holidays, I felt Erin's hand on my knee. I hadn't realised my foot was bouncing up and down and as she steadied it, she discreetly jolted her head in Alex's direction. She willed me to join in with the conversation, but I shook my head, just as discreetly declining.

'I miss family Christmases,' Joyce said. 'Instead of a cruise, it would have been nice to fly out to Australia to spend time with Nial. But Richard doesn't do aeroplanes. Which I suppose is a good job. With no guarantee of keeping Richard out of the kitchen, why spoil their day too?'

I sucked on the straw of my White Christmas Mojito. Compared to everyone else's drink, mine appeared to be vanishing at pace and I put my glass down, giving the others a chance to catch up. Listening to Joyce and Alex, it wasn't that I didn't want to include myself in their discussion. I just knew everything I said would sound contrived; nothing like the easy interaction I usually enjoyed.

Joyce suddenly fell silent and narrowed her eyes. 'You're quiet all of a sudden, Hattie.'

I should have known her gossip antennae would activate, and I made another grab for my glass. 'Just enjoying my drink.'

She looked around the group, suspicious. 'What have I missed?'

'Actually, Joyce,' Erin said, jumping in. 'I wondered if I could have a quiet word.'

'Oh no,' Joyce said, shaking her head. 'We're not doing that again.'

Ignoring her protests, Erin indicated the door. 'A quiet and very private word.'

Joyce looked from me to Alex and like any good bloodhound, she knew when she was onto something. 'You may as well tell me.'

Erin rose to her feet and taking Joyce's arm, hauled her into a standing position.

'What about my cocktail?'

Erin picked it up and shoved it into her hand. 'Happy now?'

'This is the second time you've hoicked me off,' Joyce said. She eyed everyone present. 'Someone better start talking.'

Erin looked to me, her eyebrows raised as if asking what she should do.

Joyce's tenacity knew no bounds and realising I had no choice but to relent, I nodded, giving Erin the go-ahead to explain.

Erin gestured to the door. 'Now will you come with me?'

Joyce stopped resisting and led the way.

Left to our own devices, Alex again glanced over at the bar, but he was evidently too polite to cut and run. Not that I blamed him for wanting to escape. The mixed signals I'd sent had to be as confusing to him as they were to me; Alex probably thought I was some sort of tease.

Our eyes met and knowing one of us had to say something, I drank a bit more mojito for Dutch courage. 'So how've you been since...?' Referring to our almost-kiss, my cheeks flushed. Cringing, I wanted to kick myself for drawing attention to the very thing we'd been avoiding.

'Fine. And you?'

'Fine.'

Quiet descended once more, and while Alex played with his

hands, I again picked up my glass. I drew hard on the straw creating a long loud slurp. Horrified, I froze.

Alex's face broke into a smile and relieved the ice between us had finally broken, I relaxed too.

'You should have done that sooner,' Alex said.

I chuckled, wishing I had.

Alex looked down at his hands again and taking a deep breath, he exhaled as if preparing to speak.

I could tell from his expression that, like me, he'd been thinking and knew what had to be done. As he tried to conjure the right words, having planned on saying the same thing I thought it only right I save him the embarrassment. 'I agree,' I said, jumping in first.

Alex squared his shoulders. 'I think it's for the best.'

Taking in his deep brown eyes, strong jaw and perfect lips, I nodded. Alex moving into the flat might have been a great idea in theory, but in practice it would have been impossible. Just looking at him stirred something in me and after our two close calls, I couldn't trust myself to keep my distance for a third time. 'Me too.'

Again, we fell silent, and my brain scrambled for something to say.

'Are you all ready for Christmas?' Alex asked.

'I don't have much to do now we're going to Gideon's parents' house.'

'I see.'

A look that I couldn't decipher flashed across Alex's face and I winced. Considering Gideon's behaviour towards the man in front of me, I should have been more sensitive.

Alex chewed on his lip as if deliberating something and opening his mouth to speak, he fell quiet again. Observing him, I felt saddened. The Alex I'd got to know was confident. Words came easy. Nothing about him had been hesitant.

He suddenly gathered himself and leaning forward in his seat, he placed his arms on the table. He looked at me direct. 'I need to say something.'

As he held my gaze, the seriousness in his eyes was both scary and exciting. My heart, along with the butterflies playing havoc in my tummy, wanted to hear what was on Alex's mind. They willed him to tell me I was making a mistake. That Gideon wasn't the man for me, he was. 'Please don't,' I said.

Alex stared at me, his eyes narrowing as if he was weighing up my request. His shoulders slumped. 'Okay,' he said, his voice gentle. He regarded me for a moment longer, and giving the table a quick double tap, he straightened himself up. Alex indicated the bar. 'I should get back to it.'

Rising to his feet, he picked up my empty glass. Stepping away from the table, he paused, as if needing to take one last look at me. 'Friends?' he asked.

I smiled and nodded. 'Friends.'

CHAPTER 29

CHRISTMAS EVE

I stuck the last piece of Sellotape onto the sewing kit I'd wrapped for Ewan. I wouldn't normally gift wrap items, but seeing the six-year old's eyes light up made the extra service worth it. 'There you go,' I said, handing the package to him.

Ewan looked to his dad. 'Do you think Mum will like it?'

Aiden grinned. 'She'll love it.' He turned his attention to me. 'Thanks for this. We'd have made a complete mess of it.' He ruffled the little boy's hair. 'Wouldn't we, Ewan?'

I took in the pair of them. There was no denying they were father and son. They wore identical, black-framed glasses, matching bobble hats that sat too far back from their foreheads, and both their coat collars were stuck up at one side.

It was hard not to smile as I pictured the duo attempting the task themselves. Ewan with his tongue out as he concentrated on a paper fold. Aiden, all fingers and thumbs, trying and failing to position lengths of tape in just the right place. Holding it up to assess their efforts, the result was a chaotic mess of a gift. I couldn't imagine anything more adorable. 'I'm sure you'd have managed.' Noting their matching scuffed shoes, I shook my head with a chuckle as I followed them to the exit.

'Merry Christmas,' they said as Aiden took Ewan's hand and they went on their way.

I checked my watch as I waved them off and seeing it was 5pm, I locked the door. The shop had been mad busy all day thanks to the rush of last-minute Christmas shoppers, and as I flipped the open sign to closed, I looked forward to a few days off.

I was keen to start my Yuletide break with Gideon. His parents' house might not have been my first choice of festive venue, but for our relationship's sake, I was determined to make the most of it. 'Christmas, here we come,' I said.

Upstairs, I popped my head into the lounge. Observing the madness of my vibrant and joyful tree, I recalled Christmases past when Gran and I would race into the room and ransack the pile of presents sat below its branches. Clocking the stack of board games, it saddened me to think they wouldn't get played. I'd been looking forward to a romantic evening of Baileys and backgammon. Turning my attention to the stockings on the mantel, I sighed. When it came to *l'amour*, festive or otherwise, I doubted Serena would appreciate us canoodling by her fire.

I supposed on the plus side, everything would still be there to enjoy in the new year. Something to look forward to after all the oohing and ah-ing I was about to partake in. I frowned at the growing lump of anxiety in the pit of my stomach, already dreading what might follow *The Atkins Diet for Beginners*.

Remember it's your Christmas too, Gran said.

Realising she was right, a mischievous smile spread across my lips. If I was going to be part of the Mayhew family there was no reason why I couldn't transplant some of my own traditions. I raced over and grabbed the box of Connect 4, along with the tatty primary school crown that sat with it. I smiled. 'Let the games begin.'

I jolted my head at the sound of laughter coming from the kitchen. Curious as to what was so funny, I headed across the landing to find out. Gideon was still chuckling when I entered the room and intrigued, I watched him scroll on his phone.

Sensing my presence, he hastily placed it face down on the table and began tapping on his laptop keyboard. 'It's not that time already, is it?' he asked, as I placed the board game down next to him.

My gaze went from him to my to-do list on the counter. Having landed at mine earlier than planned, Gideon had promised to get started on it. 'I thought you'd finished work until new year?'

Gideon continued to type. 'I've been asked to finalise a report, but it's taking forever.'

I shook my head, tempted to point out time wasted playing on his phone won't have helped. Switching on the radio, Boney M's 'Mary's Boy Child' rang out, and I sang along as I opened the fridge and pulled out what I needed to make our travel picnic.

'At this rate, I wouldn't be surprised if we miss the train.'

Being the last service out, that was not an option. I fell silent mid-lyric, and scowling, I turned to face Gideon. 'Then you better hurry up because we can't stay here. Unless you want a plate of chips for Christmas dinner.'

Gideon grimaced and put a hand on his tummy. 'I'm not sure my stomach's ready for all the trimmings anyway. I can't seem to get over whatever concoction Richard put in front of me.'

I eyed the half empty digestive biscuit packet on the table next to his computer. 'Nothing to do with those then?' I indicated the ham sandwiches I was about to prepare. 'Mayonnaise or mustard?'

'I'm wondering if I might be better heading back to mine. You know, give the whole Christmas thing a miss.'

Butter knife in hand, I glared at Gideon, not quite believing what I was hearing.

'Feeling the way I do, it's not like I'm going to be much company. Plus I don't know when I'll finish this.' He nodded to his laptop.

Fully aware of how much I loved Christmas, pain or no pain, work or no work, my boyfriend had to be joking. 'Your parents are expecting both of us, Gideon. It's not like I can turn up on my own.'

'I'm not suggesting you go without me.'

'Then what *are* you suggesting?' Putting the knife down, I leaned my back against the kitchen counter and folded my arms. 'That I spend Christmas here? On my own.'

'No. I just...' Gideon turned sheepish. 'Forget about it. Don't worry. I'll be fine.' His mobile vibrated, signalling a call coming through. As it rattled against the table surface, Gideon let it ring.

'Aren't you going to answer that?' I asked.

Picking it up, he checked the screen. Rubbing his forehead, he sighed. 'I don't think I should.' He looked at the caller ID for a second time. 'It's work.'

I rolled my eyes. 'You may as well go ahead. I can see you're dying to.' I gave him a stern look. 'But...' I said, stopping him from hitting the button. '...you quit with all this rubbish about cancelling Christmas and forget your stomach until after Boxing Day.'

He sighed. 'Deal.' He gestured to the landing. 'I'll take it out there.'

I snapped off the radio hoping to listen in, but Gideon's voice was muffled. Straining to hear, while I couldn't catch his words, his tone was clearly short and snappy. Considering it was after office hours on Christmas Eve, his irritation was hardly surprising and wondering what could be so important, I tiptoed over to the door to properly eavesdrop.

'You can't expect me to...' Gideon said.

With the door slightly ajar, I peeked through the gap to see him pacing up and down.

'That's easy for you to say...' He stopped still. 'I know I've had plenty of time but...'

Listening to him try and get a word in, my heart went out to Gideon. I knew he'd said his bosses were forever breathing down his neck, but from what I could hear their attitude bordered on bullying. After all the hours he'd put in of late, I hated the fact they expected more. I closed my eyes as guilt enveloped me. I hated the fact that I hadn't believed him when he'd said he'd been working late.

'I'll do it in the new year.' Grimacing, Gideon fast pulled the phone away from his ear, making it clear the caller had raised their voice. Gideon put the receiver back to his ear. 'I get that. I just don't know what else to say.' Looking pained, he ran a hand through his hair. 'Look, I've got to go. I'll speak to you in a few days.'

Secretly cheering Gideon on for sticking up for himself, I raced back to my position at the counter before he caught me spying. I flicked the radio back on. 'Everything okay?' I asked, playing innocent as Gideon re-entered the room.

'Sorry?' He pulled himself together. 'Er, yes. I'm fine.'

He didn't look fine. He looked ashen.

'It's that report I mentioned,' he said, still half distracted. 'Like I said, they wanted it sooner rather than later.'

CHAPTER 30

I turned the car radio on, hoping a few Christmas tunes would bring forth Gideon's Christmas spirit.

He reached for the off switch and silenced it again.

To hide my dismay, I turned my attention to what was going on outside the vehicle and while Gideon frowned at the road ahead, I stared out of the side window.

I stole a glance at him. Should I have gone with his suggestion that I spend the holidays alone in the flat? Gideon's work call had left his mood far from festive. While I might not have had a fridge full of treats to enjoy, lounging on the sofa, watching a Christmas special on TV, with nothing but a chip sandwich to eat, seemed way more fun.

I sighed, realising how selfish I was being. I'd heard for myself how awful Gideon's boss had been and for all I knew, Gideon could have been threatened with the sack over the expected report. Under that circumstance, it was no wonder he was brooding. I would be too. I reached over and stroked his arm. 'Are you sure you're okay?'

Gideon hands tightened around the steering wheel. 'I've told you. Everything's fine.'

My phone bleeped in a welcome diversion and pulling it from my bag, I couldn't help but smile at the photo Joyce had sent through. Its accompanying text said:

Ready for dinner. Edible food at last!

Grinning into the camera, she looked radiant in her burgundy ankle-length chiffon dress and while Richard appeared less comfortable, he cut a dashing figure in his black suit and tie. It was good to know Joyce was having fun. She deserved it. I sighed. I'd have put money on Erin having a better time than me too, despite having to prepare for her interview.

Gideon put a hand on my knee. 'I'm sorry. I'm just concentrating on the road. Once we're settled on the train and I'm finally distraction free, I promise I'll cheer up.'

I nodded, appreciating the reassurance.

I was relieved to see the train already in when we got to the station. Our Christmas Eve might not have got off to the best start, but with a bit of luck everyone else's excitement would be contagious, and Gideon would soon relax into the festive spirit.

Grabbing my tote bag and climbing out of the car, I shuddered. Having thought it cold when we'd left the flat, the air temperature seemed to have plummeted. As I moved to the rear of the vehicle, I looked up at the sky as I walked and more interested in the blanket of cloud above than what was happening on the ground, I suddenly tripped. Noticing my bootlace was undone, I crouched down in the darkness to retie it. 'Could you get my rucksack too, please,' I called out to Gideon.

He slammed the boot lid shut and the bleep from his central locking system sounded. 'I'll meet you on there,' he said, heading off.

At last following in Gideon's footsteps, I had no idea as to where our seats were. So I climbed aboard the first section of train I came to. Scanning the masses, I looked up and down the aisle in search of Gideon. With him nowhere in sight, I squeezed past luggage that fellow passengers had left in the aisle, and apologising as I went, I moved through to the next carriage.

My shoulders slumped with relief as I finally, spotted Gideon. 'There you are.' By the time I reached him, our bags were already squashed into the overhead storage rack, and he'd settled himself in.

'We were lucky,' he said, indicating our table section. 'The couple of teens that were here went back to their parents.'

I narrowed my eyes as I lowered myself into the seat opposite Gideon. 'Did they jump? Or were they pushed?'

'A bit of both,' the heavily pregnant lady in an adjacent seat replied.

Gideon frowned, while I bit down on my lips trying to hide my amusement.

The woman pulled out a book from her bag and opening it, began to read. Her face full of concentration, she had blonde hair that was tied into a ponytail, and a blunt fringe that framed her face. She wore a dark green long-sleeved jersey dress buttoned at the chest with an empire waistline that fit perfectly over her humongous pregnancy bump. I noticed a cool box ensconced in the seat opposite her and her husband, and she looked up from her book as if sensing my interest.

'Someone's come prepared,' I said.

She rubbed her belly. 'That's what happens when you're eating for two.'

Clocking the naughty glint in her eye, I immediately liked her.

Gideon pulled out his phone, his expression one of worry as he scrolled through it. He looked up as the train doors swished open, but the elderly couple that climbed aboard didn't hold his attention and he quickly got back to his screen. I shook my head in disappointment. When it came to keeping his promise, he'd have had a better chance at cheering up if he'd left his damn mobile in the car.

As they headed towards us, the elderly wife looked up and down the aisle for free seats, while her husband struggled with their suitcase. Seeing this, the father-to-be reached over and shifted the cool box out of the way to make room.

The elderly woman smiled in appreciation, as she took off her padded coat, expertly rolling it into a tight sausage as she scooted into the window seat. 'It makes the perfect pillow,' she said to the pregnant woman. 'See.' She demonstrated how it could be used to cushion her head as she leant against the glass.

Having patiently waited until his wife was settled, the elderly woman's husband tried to lift their luggage up onto the racking and watching him struggle, it was clear he needed assistance. I nudged Gideon's leg with my foot and getting his attention, willed him to step in and help.

'What?' Gideon said. Frowning, he gestured to the lack of room in the aisle, acting like there was nothing he could do.

Embarrassed by his rudeness, I was about to stand up and intervene myself, but a male voice stopped me.

'Here let me,' it said.

Closing my eyes, I cringed. *Of all the trains in all the towns in all the world, he steps onto mine.* In the commotion, I hadn't seen Alex climb aboard and watching him make room amongst the bags already stowed, my eyes darted from him to Gideon. I held my breath, hoping Gideon wouldn't look up and Alex wouldn't look down. Their prior meeting had been fraught enough. The last thing any of us needed, especially on Christmas Eve, was a rerun.

'You're a true gent,' the elderly man said, as Alex took hold of the case and scooped it into place. 'Unlike him.'

My stomach sank as, following the old man's gaze, Alex's face froze. Looking my way, his eyes met mine.

'Merry Christmas,' I said, giving him a little wave.

Alex quickly looked up and down the aisle as if searching for somewhere else to sit, but it was clear the only available spot was at our table. He appeared to contemplate his next move and realising Alex was too much of a gentleman to make things awkward, I shifted over to the window to make room for him.

'You sure you don't mind?' he asked.

It wasn't me I was worried about; it was Gideon. 'Not at all.' As far as I was concerned, Alex and I had reached a truce and agreed to be friends. 'Unless you'd rather stand?'

Alex plonked himself down and placed his bag between his feet. Staring at Gideon, he took a deep breath, in through the nose and out through the mouth.

Evidently sensing he was being watched, Gideon finally looked up from his phone and seeing Alex, his expression turned thunderous.

CHAPTER 31

The train vibrated and its engine fired up. I stared out of the window and as we pulled away leaving the station behind, civilisation turned to darkness.

Passengers throughout the carriage chatted in loud excitement. Some looked forward to catching up with family, others to their Christmas dinners. Children squealed over what they might find in their stockings, while parents looked forward to getting their little ones to bed. I looked at Gideon, who continued to appear miserable. Even without Alex's presence, I doubted that would have changed.

Needing something other than him to focus on, I reached into my tote bag and pulled out my knitting. Smoothing out the blanket I'd recently started, I was happy to lose myself in the rhythmic clickety-clack of my needles.

Obviously wanting a distraction too, Alex delved into his rucksack and produced his pencil and sketchpad. As he turned to a blank page, Gideon looked up from his phone and taking in Alex's creative tools, scowled. Not that this seemed to bother Alex. He simply set about drawing.

187

Noting Gideon's disdain, I wondered how a man could have so much dislike for someone he hardly knew. Alex's mere presence brought out an arrogance in Gideon that I didn't much care for. Whether it was the result of insecurity or not, it was a reaction I found both unnecessary and embarrassing. And dare I say it, childish.

Alex was clearly talented, and peeking at his sketch, I was amazed at how quickly he worked. I was mesmerised as I watched his pencil strokes come to life. Sweeping lines turned more detailed and once shading was introduced, a clear picture of the adjacent pregnant woman and her husband emerged.

Returning my attention to my own creative endeavour, white flakes landing on the window caught my eye. 'Look, everyone, it's snowing,' I said. In my excitement, I tapped Alex's leg and like mine, his face lit up. He leaned over for a closer look, and I breathed in the intoxicating scent of sandalwood and spices that I'd come to associate with Alex.

'Fantastic,' he said. 'We might get a white Christmas, after all.'

Gideon frowned. 'I've never understood the fuss myself.'

Alex flicked his gaze upwards as he settled himself back down. 'Sounds like someone lost a few snowball fights in his time.'

I put a hand up to my mouth to hide my amusement, while Gideon, keeping his eyes on his phone, pursed his lips.

I regarded my boyfriend, wondering if Alex might have had a point. There had to be a reason Gideon kept his inner child buried. In all the time I'd known him, he'd never daydreamed or been playful and free-spirited. From what I'd seen from his interactions with Alex, even art was to be met with scorn. I sighed. When it came to letting go, Gideon either didn't have the know-how, or as he would claim, *see the need.*

The doors to the next carriage opened and I looked over to see the train conductor step forward. Clearly a fellow fan of the festive season, he wore a Santa hat and a massive smile that reminded me of Gran's. 'Merry Christmas,' he said, as he punched and handed back tickets. 'Ho! Ho! Ho!'

He finally reached us. 'Tickets please.'

While I waited for Gideon to produce ours, Alex dug into his pocket and handed his over. With the elderly and pregnant couples holding theirs out at the ready, the conductor turned his attention to them.

'Someone's having a good evening,' the elderly woman said.

'It's my final shift,' the conductor replied. 'As of tomorrow, I'm officially retired.' He dipped his chin. 'Enough to make anyone smile, wouldn't you say?'

Thinking of Joyce, I wondered if the conductor's wife would agree.

Alex nudged me. 'How cool is that? Carrying out your last duties, on the last train before Christmas?'

Gideon rolled his eyes.

Turning his attention to the pregnant couple, the conductor punched their tickets. 'Fingers crossed the driver will put his foot down and I can start celebrating early.' He looked to Gideon and me.

As if sensing my stare, Gideon finally let his phone drop. 'What? I haven't got them. I put them in the pocket of your rucksack.'

I gave him a stiff smile and indicated the overhead storage rack. 'Then could you pass it to me please?' His behaviour was beginning to really grate.

Alex rose to his feet. 'I'll get it. What am I looking for?'

'Thank you,' I said. 'It's black. With a crocheted frog keyring on one of the straps.'

Searching through the luggage, Alex frowned. 'It doesn't seem to be here.'

Again, I turned my eyes on Gideon.

'Don't look at me,' Gideon said. 'I don't know where it is.'

Everyone was watching us. I hated being the centre of attention and my cheeks reddened. 'What are you talking about? You brought it in from the car.'

'No, I didn't.'

'Yes, you did. I asked you to grab it, remember. At the station when I was tying my lace.' I swallowed, my embarrassment fast turning to frustration. 'Please tell me you didn't leave it behind?'

Gideon shrugged. 'I must've done.'

I pictured my rucksack lying in the boot of Gideon's BMW, realising our tickets were the least of my problems. I had no toothbrush, let alone a clean set of clothes. Worse still, the Christmas cards and gifts I'd bought for his family were in that bag and I could already hear Serena's disparaging remarks at me turning up empty-handed. Seeing Gideon's nonchalance, I didn't know whether to laugh or cry.

'You'll have to buy more tickets, I'm afraid,' the conductor said.

Alex automatically dug his hand in his pocket, but the conductor stopped him.

'My purse is in my bag,' I said. 'Is there any way...'

'I'm not talking to you, love.' The conductor's face turned serious as he jerked his head in Gideon's direction. 'I'm talking to him.'

'I don't think so.' Gideon huffed as he crossed his arms. 'I'm not...'

'A gentleman?' the conductor asked, eyebrows raised.

Gideon's gaze went from him to everyone around us. People's expressions ranged from disbelief to contempt, leaving him under no illusion as to what they thought. Realising he had no choice in the matter, he finally pulled out his wallet. 'I don't believe this,' he said, holding his card over the payment machine.'

'Thank you, sir,' the conductor said. 'That wasn't hard was it.' He handed our new tickets to me, and with a smile and a wink went on his way.

I pulled out my phone and hit Google. If I could find a shop that was open on Christmas Day, hopefully one of Gideon's family members would drive me so I could at least brush my teeth. As my search continued, my heart sank. It appeared I was stuck until Boxing Day.

The train slowed, and numerous passengers got up from their seats. I watched them excitedly gather up their belongings ready for their festive celebrations to start in earnest. Feeling envious, I wished they'd take me with them. I sighed. If I'd thought the previous Christmas was bad enough, it was nothing compared to what I was currently going through.

Turning my attention to outside the window, my eyes widened. A continuous flurry of huge snowflakes cascaded to the ground and as the train came to a standstill, the whole platform was a blanket of white. The perfect canvas for snow angels and footprint patterns, the station was like a Christmas card scene. Children squealed in delight as they and their families disembarked. Scooping up handfuls of snow, they shaped them into balls and threw them in all directions. Smiling as I watched them, I wondered how many were already planning to build snowmen.

'This is cosy, isn't it?' the elderly woman said. She gestured to the empty carriage. 'Looks like we're the only ones left.' She smiled at each of us. 'I'm Martha, by the way. And this is Brian.'

'Alex.' He reached over and shook everyone's hands. 'Nice to meet you.'

'Lexi,' the pregnant woman said. She indicated her husband. 'This is Jake.'

All eyes turned to me.

'Hattie.' I looked to my boyfriend, but he was still more interested in his phone. 'That's Gideon.'

Alex eyed the rows of vacant seats. He turned to me. 'Actually, I might just...'

Nodding, I appreciated why Alex would want to move. The journey so far hadn't exactly been joyful. Another look at Gideon and I felt tempted to go with him.

Alex was halfway to his feet when the carriage doors swished open. Clocking the arrival of a new passenger, his eyes widened, and he dropped back down.

Wondering why he'd lost the use of his legs, I followed his gaze. My head flinched back slightly and I frowned. *What's she doing here?* I wondered if I was imagining things: Julia was the last person I expected to see.

As she approached, I supposed Alex's response wasn't surprising; Julia looked stunning. Stylish as ever, she wore a Barbour jacket in classic olive, knee-high boots and, as was customary, perfect make-up. Carrying what was clearly an expensive travel bag, she swapped it from one leather-gloved hand to her other.

Her presence couldn't be a coincidence.

'Gideon,' I said, not taking my eyes off Julia. 'What's going on?'

'What do you mean?'

I indicated over his shoulder and following my eyeline, Gideon twisted round in his seat. Curious as to what all the fuss was about, Martha, Brian, Lexi and Jake followed suit. I shook my head in disdain as Julia revelled in the attention. Anyone would have thought the train aisle was her personal catwalk.

She took off her beanie and flicking her head, ran her fingers through her long lustrous hair. Removing what I knew from experience was a luxury angora scarf, a delicious smile spread across her face. 'There you are, Gideon,' she said, placing her bag on the now empty seat behind him. 'Didn't I tell you we'd be on the same train.' She raised her eyebrows. 'Now be a darling and make some room. I'd like to sit down.'

CHAPTER 32

Questions swirled through my mind as to the reasons behind Julia's presence, but preferring to hold on to my dignity, I refused to demand answers or make a scene. Trying to pretend all was well, I smiled at the two couples on the adjacent table. But my acting was clearly below par as their curiosity appeared to continue.

As Julia slid into her seat, she positioned herself closer to Gideon than she could have done were we on an aeroplane. Not that Gideon seemed to notice. He didn't even try and inch himself away. Her confident gaze went from me to Alex, and she narrowed her eyes as if weighing him up. She cocked her head. 'Do I know you?'

Alex smiled. 'I don't know. Do you?'

Despite my discomfort, I chuckled at his mischievousness.

'I'm sure I've seen you somewhere before.'

'He has one of those faces,' I said. 'Once seen, never forgotten.'

'Why thank you,' Alex replied with a grin. 'I'm taking that as a compliment.'

Gideon coughed as if reminding us he was there. A gesture I thought a bit rich, considering his and Julia's thighs were touching.

'No. It's more than that.' With a look of concentration, Julia continued to search her memory bank. 'Don't worry. It'll come to me.'

'Julia, can I have a word please?' Gideon suddenly asked.

Surprising all of us, he was up on his feet before she could answer.

She raised her eyebrows. 'As long as it's not work-related.'

Wondering what was going on, I raised mine too. 'What else would it be?'

Gideon struggled to hide his irritation. At who, it was hard to tell. 'It's about that report I mentioned,' he said, his voice strained. 'While it's still on my mind.'

Julia rolled her eyes and stepping out into the aisle, gestured for Gideon to lead the way.

Martha and Lexi craned their necks to observe Gideon and Julia, but as my boyfriend and his colleague made sure they were far enough away to prevent any eavesdropping, the two women's curiosity was disappointed. As their shoulders slumped, Martha and Lexi looked to each other then turned to me, their expressions reloaded with intrigue.

'Are you okay?' Alex asked. Leaning my way, he kept his voice low.

With the atmosphere at our table chillier than the winter temperatures, I understood Martha and Lexi's interest. In their shoes, I'd probably want the lowdown too. Mustering the best smile I could, I nodded at Alex. 'I'm fine, thank you.'

Gideon and Julia huddled towards each other and whatever their discussion was about I could see it was serious. Although with Gideon's back to me I could only observe Julia's contribution. Every now and then she glanced my way and wishing I could lip-read, I frowned at her. She reminded me of Serena. Quick to offer a friendly smile that was anything but.

I looked for clues that might indicate something untoward – a seductive smile here or a suggestive flick of her hair there – but none were forthcoming. Despite still having no idea why Julia was on the train, I told myself I was worrying over nothing and put my unease down to paranoia.

The train had stopped at several stations by the time Gideon and Julia deigned to rejoin us. As well as all things report-related, Gideon had obviously shared with Julia his dislike of Alex. Retaking her seat, her upper lip curled as she looked at him, such was her newfound disdain. Alex chuckled but while he might not have cared, I did. Gideon had no right to bad-mouth anyone like that.

Gideon jerked his head. 'What's going on? Why are we slowing down?' He glanced out of the window. 'There's no platform coming up.'

Putting my hand up to the glass, I leaned in and peered out into the darkness. Much like my mood, the snow had got heavier. Squinting into the distance, all I could see were fields upon fields of white. Any other Christmas Eve and it would have delighted me.

The doors to the next carriage opened and the conductor appeared. 'Nothing to worry about, ladies and gentlemen.' The train came to an abrupt stop, almost knocking him off his feet. His Santa hat slid to one side, and he grabbed a headrest to steady himself. 'It's just a minor delay.' He tidied himself up. 'We'll be on our way again soon.'

While the conductor headed back the way he came, Martha's face lit up. 'How exciting. It's like we're on the Orient Express.'

Her husband Brian nodded in our direction. 'As long as

there's no murder,' he said. The frostiness around our table had obviously crossed the aisle into their territory.

'What do we do now?' Lexi asked, a big smile on her face.

'Wait it out, I suppose,' Jake replied.

'We could always eat.' Lexi rubbed her humongous belly. 'Me and little bean could do with a snack.'

Julia snorted but as she opened her mouth to say something Alex jumped in before she could speak. 'When's the baby due?' he asked.

'Not for another four weeks,' Lexi replied. 'And counting.'

'Hence, our Christmas break,' Jake said. Looking to his wife, he took her hand. 'Our last hurrah, just the two of us.' In a moment of sweetness, he appeared to lose himself in her gaze. Snapping himself out of it, he returned his attention to the group. 'We thought we'd make the most of it.'

Lexi giggled. 'I wasn't up for it at first. Then I thought why *not* let someone else do the running around for a change.'

'Why not, indeed,' Martha said. 'You'll have your hands full soon enough.'

Alex laughed. 'I can second that if my nieces and nephew are anything to go by.'

'I third it,' Brian said. 'Our grandkids have got energy like you wouldn't believe.'

Listening to them, I felt an ache in my chest, wishing I could fourth it.

Lexi turned serious. 'Oh no, our baby won't be a struggle. This pregnancy has been an absolute dream.' She nudged her husband. 'Hasn't it, Jake?'

Jake's smile tightened. 'It sure has.'

'A perfect bean on the inside makes for a perfect bean out,' Lexi said. 'That's what I say.' She waved a dismissive hand. 'There'll be none of this crying all the time and sleepless nights business.' Lexi wrinkled her nose and again turned to her husband. 'About that food...'

Jake sprung into action. 'Yes, sorry.' Opening their cool box, he produced two large jars and unscrewing their lids, placed both in front of his wife.

The rest of us looked on in horror as Lexi took a gherkin from one and dipped it into the chocolate spread contained in the other.

My jaw dropped and I put a hand up to my chest as she stuffed the gherkin into her mouth.

Lexi was clearly in gourmet heaven, and as she savoured the taste, Alex tried not to gag.

I wondered if, like Richard, she had no palate, or if she was simply experiencing some weird pregnancy craving. Regardless, as she chomped on her snack, the pickled gherkin sounded way better than it looked.

'Can you pass me the squirty cream?' Lexi asked her husband.

Alex quickly looked away.

'I think we'll join you,' Martha said.

Brian almost choked.

His wife rolled her eyes. 'I was referring to our sandwiches.'

Relieved, Brian retrieved their rucksack from the storage rack above his head and pulling out a tin foiled parcel, handed it to her.

Gideon huffed. 'We could have eaten too if someone hadn't forgotten their bag.'

Unable to believe he'd just said that, I glowered at his selfishness. 'Think yourself lucky. I don't even have clean knickers.'

Julia leaned into Gideon. 'I'm beginning to see what you mean.'

Having clearly overheard, Martha and Lexi gasped, while I looked from Julia to my boyfriend.

'Gideon, what's she talking about?' I asked, as he shifted in his seat.

As if I hadn't spoken, Julia patted his arm. 'How does avocado, grilled halloumi and a smoky chipotle sauce sound?'

'Bloody awful,' Brian said.

Julia got to her feet and grabbed her travel bag. Sticking her nose in the air, she ignored Brian's quip and headed for an alternative table. 'There's more than enough here for two,' she said, making it clear Alex and I were not invited.

I scoffed, pitying the woman her confidence. Hungry or not, no way was Gideon about to accept her offer. I folded my arms and with a smug smile, looked forward to seeing Julia dine alone.

Gideon rose from his seat.

My eyes widened and my smile vanished. 'What are you doing?'

He shrugged. 'What can I say? I'm hungry.'

I shot forward in my seat, my cheeks burning with embarrassment as I watched him go. Wondering how he could humiliate me in front of everyone like that, I wanted nothing more than to take Julia's smoky chipotle sauce and rub it in Gideon's face. Feeling everyone's eyes on me, I again tried to maintain a sense of decorum. Heat coursed through my veins and determined to control my anger, I swallowed hard. It didn't work; I still wanted to kill Gideon. 'Excuse me please,' I said to Alex, working hard to control my tone.

Alex's face turned pallid as I picked up my knitting needles and stood up.

'Don't worry,' I said, stuffing them into my tote bag. 'I'm only going to find the buffet cart.'

As Alex manoeuvred himself out of my way, he paused to

glare at Gideon and Julia. But I didn't want Alex's sympathy, I just wanted to get away before I did something to get me arrested.

Stepping out onto the aisle, tears pricked my eyes, but I refused to let them fall. Unable to bring myself to look at anyone, I simply stared straight ahead and holding my breath, walked away.

CHAPTER 33

Entering the next train carriage, I realised I couldn't buy myself something to eat even if I'd really wanted to. My purse was in my rucksack in the boot of Gideon's car.

Plonking myself down on the first seat I came to, I swiped at my eyes, refusing to let Gideon's selfishness reduce me to tears. I wished more than ever that I'd stayed at home. Christmas alone was way better than the situation I'd found myself in.

I was damned if I was spending it with Gideon. He had humiliated me beyond belief. But as I put my elbows on my knees and dropped my head into my hands, I knew I didn't have a choice. With no train back and nowhere to go, without Gideon, I was stranded.

Recalling Erin's offer to spend Christmas with her, I straightened myself up and reaching into my bag for my mobile, brought up her number. I was sure if I rang and explained, Erin wouldn't hesitate to come and collect me. Desperate for help, I pressed the call button and waited for her to answer.

As the ring tone continued, I chewed on the inside of my cheek, picturing Erin and her mum Maeve settled in front of the

TV. Erin had already explained how much Maeve loved the King's College Choir. The two of them watching Carols from King's with a bottle of Baileys was a Christmas Eve tradition clearly too important to interrupt.

Taking the phone away from my ear, I ended the call, but my thumb hovered as I considered trying again. Aware that Erin's interview preparations already impinged on their celebrations, it didn't seem fair of me to encroach on her and Maeve further. I sighed and letting my thumb land, swiped the screen clear instead.

Resigned to putting up with Gideon until at least Boxing Day, I put my mobile away again and shifting over to the window seat, pulled my coat tight across my chest. I leant my head against the glass. 'Merry Christmas, Hattie,' I said to my reflection, feeling sorry for myself.

The carriage doors swished open, and Alex appeared. He dumped his rucksack on the floor and sitting down next to me, placed his pencil and pad in the space between us. 'I wanted to make sure you're all right,' he said.

I scoffed. 'Shouldn't that be Gideon's job?'

Alex's expression remained deadpan. 'I don't think he can move because of his full belly.'

I burst out laughing, Alex's humour being just what I needed. 'Thank you,' I said, as we both sat chuckling.

'For what?'

'For being you.' I shifted round to face him. 'How do you do it?'

Alex looked at me bemused.

'It's like you've got this innate ability to lighten a mood. To make things seem better.'

Alex shrugged. 'Lots of practice, I suppose.'

I rolled my eyes. 'Don't tell me. Being the only man in a house full of women is...'

'Character building? An endurance test? You wouldn't believe the dramas I've been privy to.'

I looked at Alex direct. 'Is that what you think I'm being? Dramatic.'

'Nope. You should be proud of yourself. You showed great restraint back there.' Alex held my gaze, but whatever he was thinking, he shook himself out of it. 'You must be starving by now.' He placed his hands on his knees as if getting ready to move. 'Why don't I go and see if I can find some food?'

I gathered myself too. 'I couldn't face anything. My appetite's gone.'

'A coffee then? Who knows how long we're going to be stuck in this snow.' He stood up. 'The caffeine might come in handy.'

Watching him head off, I appreciated Alex's presence. He didn't have to look out for me; he'd chosen to. Unlike my so-called boyfriend, who was too busy thinking about his own needs to consider mine. I wondered if Gideon had always been like that and thanks to my grief or some subconscious deep-rooted fear of being alone, I just hadn't seen it. I took a deep breath and exhaled. Considering my predicament, those were questions for another day.

Alex's sketch pad caught my eye and picking it up, I turned to the first page. Marvelling at Alex's artistic ability, it was hard to believe he hadn't been to art school.

Flicking through it, I smiled at a picture of Ted who, pint in hand, sat at the bar in The Royal Oak. The deep wrinkles in his forehead, his bushy grey eyebrows and permanent frown... Every aspect of his face was drawn in such detail, I could have been forgiven for thinking I was looking at a photograph.

My heart melted as I landed on a sketch of me, Erin and Joyce, obviously drawn at one of our recent Crochet Club meet-ups. It was a perfect representation of the three of us. Joyce, with her woeful expression, had to be complaining about Richard, while Erin, holding a glass in one hand and pointing a finger with the other, was, without doubt, talking about Callum. I put a hand up to my head, frowning as I homed in on myself. Looking at the state of my hair, Alex clearly didn't believe in artistic licence.

Each drawing was signed and dated and image after image, the pad was like a pictorial diary of Alex's life and the people he came across.

Flipping through the pages my breath suddenly caught, and my hand stopped still. I took in the couple before me. Him, eyes glistening and expression playful. Her, arm outstretched on the table so that their hands almost touched. It's often said that every picture tells a story, and Alex had demonstrated this one all too clearly. Absorbing every last detail, I even knew the location – Le Bonsoir. A place so expensive that despite us going Dutch, Gideon refused to set foot in the place again. My pulse raced. Yet there he was committed to paper with Julia.

My eyes fell on the date the sketch was drawn. Unable to believe my stupidity, it was the night we'd arranged to see the special cinema screening of *It's a Wonderful Life*. I'd fallen for his lie about having to work late and sat alone in the theatre, swallowing my disappointment, trying to convince myself that Gideon's absence didn't matter. My heart pounded. Out wining and dining, oh, how the two of them must have laughed at me.

When it came to Gideon, it seemed my foolishness knew no bounds and I let the sketch pad drop as realisation dawned. My eyes widened. Gideon's behaviour towards Alex wasn't a result of jealousy. It came from a place of fear. Gideon was scared Alex might reveal his and Julia's secret.

My body tensed as my mind flashed back to Copington Christmas Market. Julia hadn't been there to help choose a gift; the two of them had been on a date. But that wasn't Gideon's worst sin that night. I remembered his words about how I'd said

I wouldn't go there again after Gran had died. A vow he undoubtedly banked on, I suddenly felt sick. Not content with lying to my face, he'd used my grief to get away with playing around behind my back.

Recalling his sincerity at the restaurant, I scowled. Gideon had tried to be manipulative then too. The fuss he'd made about him being logical and me creative. It was no wonder I'd misunderstood the situation. Maybe if he hadn't patronised me, talked in a way that suggested opposites attract, I wouldn't have anticipated a proposal. He should have got straight to the point and dumped me.

He'd shown the same gutlessness when he'd waxed lyrical about where best to celebrate Christmas. Gideon knew he hadn't invited me to his parents. An assumption on my part, I'd inserted myself into an environment where nobody, including him, wanted me. I glanced down at the sketch of Gideon and Julia. Yet he said nothing.

Picturing Gideon as he paced up and down my landing during his earlier phone call, I scoffed. Kudos to him for thinking on his feet. Reports to finish, expectant bosses on the phone, I'd had no idea it was Julia, the woman he clearly planned on spending Christmas with, on the other end of the line. Gideon certainly had me fooled.

Heat raced through my veins. That's why she was there on the train. She was letting Gideon know she would no longer stay in the shadows.

A part of me wanted to believe Julia wouldn't be that cruel. That she didn't really expect him to leave me, in the middle of nowhere, on Christmas Eve. But envisaging her smug smile as she walked down the train aisle ready to claim her man, I scowled. Of course she did.

Looking back, it was easy to see how pathetic and gullible I'd been. How I should have listened to my inner voice that kept insisting all was not as it seemed. But unlike Gideon, at least I wasn't a coward. Neither was my ego so big that I needed to come out of every situation looking like the good guy.

Taking a deep breath to steady myself, a coldness came over me and I got up from my seat ready to face everyone.

CHAPTER 34

*A*rms by my side, I stood, gathering myself ready to challenge Gideon and Julia. In through my nose and out through my mouth, I slowly inhaled and exhaled. Despite the breathing exercise, my heart pounded. 'You've got this,' I said. Clenching my hand, I used the side of my fist to hit the *carriage open* button and stepping forward, I marched in their direction.

Gideon and Julia were back in their original seats and fixing a smile on my face, I kept my eyes on them as I sat down opposite.

Martha tapped me on my arm. 'I saved you a sandwich.' She glowered at Gideon as she handed me the last of her tinfoil wrapped parcel and seeing her displeasure, I wondered how she'd react if she knew Gideon had done more than eat with the woman next to him.

'You need something in your tummy,' Lexi said. Pacing up and down the aisle, she grimaced as she rubbed her belly, having obviously eaten too many chocolate-flavoured gherkins. 'Goodness knows how long we're going to be here.'

'It's probably a snowdrift,' Jake said.

Brian laughed. 'A leaf on the track, more like.'

While they chatted about the problems with the rail operator, I focused my attention on Julia. The train's stark lighting wasn't doing her any favours. Her make-up didn't appear as refined, and I was sure there were a couple of grey strands in her otherwise dark hair. Correcting myself, I refused to behave like the woman before me. Attaching the flaws in her character to her appearance might serve my anger, but I was better than that.

Julia shifted in her seat, as if pretending not to notice my stare.

I chuckled. She wasn't that good an actress.

I wondered how she and Gideon planned to resolve our festive threesome. Julia was clearly a *pick me* kind of woman, but in forcing Gideon's hand, underneath all her glamour and bravado she couldn't one-hundred per cent believe Gideon would choose her. After all, he hadn't so far.

I tilted my head. 'So where are you off to, Julia?'

'I, er...' She looked from me to Gideon, lost for words. I almost felt sorry for her. The desperation in her eyes was pitiful.

Gideon squirmed. He clearly wanted all the benefits of an affair, but none of the responsibility. That could explain why he'd accepted Julia's food offering so readily. One word from her wouldn't just make public his behaviour; it would make him outwardly accountable.

I sneered. He'd probably hoped I'd make a scene. Give him a reason to dump me in a way that enabled him and Julia to cast me as the bad guy and them the victims. After all, he had form. In leaving my bag in the car, wasn't I the one who'd left him hungry? I scoffed. Innocent was the last thing those two were.

'Everything okay?' Gideon asked, clearly sensing something was afoot.

'Why wouldn't it be?' As his eyes darted towards the carriage doors, I knew he was questioning Alex's whereabouts. Panicking over what we had or hadn't talked about when we were out of sight, let alone earshot.

Seeing his discomfort a warmth radiated through my body. Oh, how the tables had turned.

Gideon swallowed. 'You just seem a bit on edge.' He pulled at his collar.

Ignoring his observation, I indicated his phone with a smile. 'You might want to text your mum to let her know we're running late. There's no point her sitting on a cold station platform, when she could be keeping that gorgeous inglenook burning for us.'

As Julia flashed Gideon a look, the carriage doors opened, and Alex appeared. Rucksack slung over his shoulder, he carried two takeaway cups of coffee. 'There you go.' Handing me one of the drinks, he lowered himself into his seat. As if sensing the shift in atmosphere, he glanced around the group.

'Well, this is nice, isn't it?' I said.

Martha shuddered. 'I don't know about that. It's getting a bit chilly in here?'

Brian nodded in our direction. 'It's colder on that side of the aisle.'

Still pacing, Lexi rubbed her belly. 'I shouldn't have eaten so much.' She grimaced at the two empty jars on the table where she'd sat. 'I've got indigestion.'

I chuckled, seizing the opportunity to humiliate my boyfriend like he had me. 'Reminds me of the time you were rushed to hospital, Gideon.'

Gideon glared at me. 'I don't think that's an event worth sharing, do you?'

Turning to the rest of the group, I couldn't have disagreed more. 'He was convinced he was having a heart attack and insisted I ring him an ambulance. Of course, with all his moaning and groaning, I was straight on the phone. The paramedics weren't taking any chances either. They raced him to A&E.'

I could still feel my panic as I floored Beryl's accelerator trying to follow the flashing blue light. My fear was overwhelming as I sat in the hospital car park, hands glued to the steering wheel, willing myself to get out of the van and run to Gideon's side. By the time I'd talked myself into it and pulled my keys out of the ignition Gideon was lowering himself into the passenger seat desperate to get away from there.

Lexi's eyes widened. 'What happened?'

I looked at Gideon. 'Do you want to tell them or shall I?'

His cheeks reddened, while his cold stare told me he'd deal with me later.

'Nothing,' I said, keeping my eyes on him. 'It was trapped wind.'

Alex sniggered, rattling Gideon more so.

'Perhaps you could let Lexi have some of your Gaviscon.' I returned my attention back to everyone else. 'He always keeps a bottle with him. Despite not having *any* shame, even he doesn't want to suffer humiliation like that again.'

Gideon opened his mouth to speak, but I wouldn't let him.

'You know what we should do?' I said. 'Play charades.'

'Hell, yes.' Lexi's discomfort vanished as she speed-waddled back to her seat. She tapped Jake's leg in excitement.

'It's not like we have anything else to do,' Martha said, equally enthusiastic.

Gideon sighed.

'Oh, come on,' I said. 'Don't be such a spoil sport.' Again, I turned to the group. 'If there's one thing I've learned about this man, it's that he loves to play games.'

Gideon lowered his voice. 'I don't know what's got into you, but...'

'But what, Gideon?' I asked, raising mine.

'I'm in,' Alex said. Ready to go, he smiled at my so-called boyfriend.

'I'll go first.' I rose to my feet by the window and making sure everyone could see me, I mimed holding a video camera.

'It's a film,' Lexi said.

I held up my middle and index fingers.

'Two words,' Martha said.

I wiggled one of them.

'First word,' everyone except Gideon and Julia called out.

I clutched my chest and pretended to keel over.

'Indigestion!' Lexi said.

All but Gideon and Julia burst out laughing.

Getting back to the game, I continued to mime, and everyone's answers came thick and fast.

'Dead.'

'Faint.'

'Passed.'

With none of them correct, I paused to think. I picked up my coffee cup and taking a swig, put it down while pretending I was choking on it.

'Poisonous,' Alex said.

I pointed to the cup.

'Fatal!' Jake said.

Nodding, I held up two fingers.

'Second word,' Lexi said.

I turned to Alex and swooned.

'*Fatal Attraction!*' Martha said.

I touched my nose and pointed at her. As Martha congratulated herself, I turned to Gideon and Julia. 'I'm surprised neither of you got that.' Wrinkling my nose, I gave them a patronising smile. 'Not to worry, I've got another one.' Picking up my imaginary video camera, I started again.

'Film,' Alex said.

I held up a finger.

'One word,' Martha said.

I pointed to Gideon and then to myself.

'Couple,' Lexi said. 'Married. Together.' She was clearly determined to win the round.

'Boyfriend. Girlfriend,' Martha said.

I pretended to cry and pointed to Gideon and Julia.

The two of them looked back at me horrified.

Jake jumped to his feet. '*Unfaithful!*'

There was an immediate silence, and as all eyes turned to Gideon and Julia, Jake slowly sat down.

'Well done, Jake,' I said, keeping my eyes fixed on them too. 'That's exactly what it is.'

CHAPTER 35

Continuing to stare at Gideon and Julia, everyone sat in stunned silence.

'Didn't I tell you there was something funny about that lot,' Brian said.

Martha shushed him, clearly wanting answers as much as I did.

Gideon's gaze went from one person to the next and like a goldfish, he kept opening and closing his mouth, as if he couldn't quite articulate whatever his brain was telling him.

In contrast, Julia appeared confident. Knees together and spine poker straight, she angled her body towards Gideon. With a shake of her head, she flicked her hair.

I narrowed my eyes, wondering if she was proud of her actions, or now that everything was out in the open, simply pleased she'd finally bagged her man.

Gideon let out an exaggerated sigh. 'Whatever you think you know–'

'Please don't embarrass yourself,' I said. 'You've done enough of that already. Besides, I've seen the evidence.'

Martha turned to Brian. 'I told you it was like the Orient Express. This is the bit at the end, when Poirot reveals the truth.'

Gideon's nostrils flared. His eyes turned colder as he scowled at Alex. 'You just couldn't keep your mouth shut, could you?'

'Really?' I said, although I shouldn't have been surprised. 'That's what you're going with.' I let out a laugh. 'No *I'm sorry, Hattie. We didn't mean for this to happen.*'

'Puh-lease. Not that old chestnut,' Martha said.

'But we didn't,' Julia said, evidently affronted. 'Things between us just...'

I glowered at her. 'I wasn't talking to you.'

Gideon put a reassuring hand on hers and clearly feigning upset, Julia inched nearer to him.

'Then again, at least you're owning what you've done.' I jerked my head in Gideon's direction. 'He's just annoyed he got caught.' I looked at him direct. 'I mean, is that really the best you can do? Blame someone else for the mess you created?'

'What am I supposed to think?' With a look of contempt, he nodded Alex's way. 'He's been trying to come between us since....'

Alex appeared affronted. 'Actually...'

'Don't defend yourself, Alex. It doesn't matter what you say, you'll always be his excuse. If there's one thing I've learned, nothing's ever Gideon's fault.' I sneered. 'So, what was the plan? To dump me at the station? For Serena to keep me entertained while the two of you snuck around behind my back? Does your mother know I'm even on this train?' I mocked my own stupidity. 'It's not like I'm meant to be, is it?'

The carriage doors opened, and the conductor appeared. 'Ho! Ho! H...' His voice trailed off and his smile froze. Realising he was interrupting something, he raised a finger and opened his mouth to speak. Clearly thinking better of it, he stopped himself and taking a step back, slowly retreated out of view again.

Lexi got up from her seat. 'Don't mind me.' She winced, her earlier indigestion still plaguing her. 'I'm just gonna stretch my legs.'

Gideon leaned forward in his seat. 'Can't you see how uncomfortable you're making everyone?'

My eyes widened. 'So now you care about people's feelings?'

'Don't worry about us,' Martha said. She nodded at me. 'You carry on, love.'

Julia rolled her eyes. 'Maybe if you weren't so needy you'd have seen how unhappy Gideon was?'

'Excuse me?'

Lexi suddenly took a sharp intake of breath, but as Jake jumped to his feet, she indicated he sit down again. 'It's nothing. Probably Braxton Hicks. Like a practice contraction.' She looked to me. 'As you were.'

Jake and I hesitated, but as Lexi gestured all was well, reaffirming her desire that I continue, Jake reluctantly retook his seat, and I returned my attention to Julia. 'I don't know what Gideon has told you but...'

'He's told me about your pathetic little wool shop and about how you miss your grandmother so much you're turning into her.'

Julia's words stung and I looked to Gideon, this time hoping I would be met with denials. I wanted him to say Julia was lying. That he'd never dream of talking about me in that way. But the fact that he couldn't bring himself to even look at me, told me all I needed to know. Met with silence, my body seemed to collapse in on itself and feeling broken, I dropped into my seat. Any fight I had vanished. I suddenly felt numb.

'The only reason he didn't leave you months ago is because he felt sorry for you,' Julia carried on.

Alex shot forward. 'That's enough.'

'Now we're getting somewhere,' Gideon said. 'You're only playing the hero because you fancy her.'

'What man wouldn't?' Alex asked, incredulous.

Gideon appeared shocked.

'You didn't expect me to deny it, did you?' Alex laughed. 'I'm not blind.'

Gideon's lips curled. 'The truth always comes out.'

'Shame you didn't think about that before you started up with her.' Alex indicated Julia.

Gideon scowled. 'I always knew there was something going on between the two of you.'

'I'm sorry,' Jake suddenly said. 'But I can't listen to anymore.' He rounded on Gideon. 'Stop judging people by your standards, will you? I've never met a more arrogant, selfish individual.' He looked to Julia. 'I don't even know what to say to you. You're just cruel.'

'Hear! Hear!' Martha said.

Brian patted his wife's hand. 'You stay out of it,' he said.

Martha laughed. 'Why? The man's a buffoon.'

Lexi let out another yelp.

'Now look what you've done,' Gideon said to me.

'Jake...' Lexi said.

'I'm sorry, babe.' He scratched his forehead. 'But it needed saying.'

'No, Jake...' Panic-stricken, she slowly looked down at her feet.

Following her gaze, everyone's eyes widened at the pool of water she stood in.

CHAPTER 36

The seconds we all stood there staring at the pool of water seemed to go on forever.

'That's not what I think it is, is it?' The colour drained from Gideon's face.

'Ew,' Julia said.

Gideon's eyes began to roll, and passing out, his head landed on Julia's shoulder.

'This was not on my Christmas bingo card,' Brian said.

Finally snapping into action, I reached for my bag and fumbled for my phone. 'I'll ring for an ambulance.'

'But we're in the middle of nowhere,' Jake said. 'What if it can't find us?' He raced to the window and peering through the glass, scanned our surroundings. 'It's pitch black out there. We're miles from a station.' He looked back at us. 'I doubt there's even a road.' Fear all over his face, he put a hand up to his head. 'Think, Jake, think.'

Lexi whimpered.

'Don't worry.' Alex stepped forward, his expression one of confident reassurance. 'We have plenty of time before the baby comes. Labour might not kick in for twenty-four hours.'

Lexi appeared less than convinced. 'Which suggests it could also start sooner.'

'One step at a time,' Alex continued. 'For now, we just need to monitor your pains to see if there's a pattern to them.'

Wondering what made him the font of all midwifery knowledge, I gave him a questioning look.

'My sister had home births,' Alex said. 'You don't forget these things.'

'Did you hear that, Lexi? Alex has done this before.' Jake moved to comfort his wife.

'Don't touch me.' She glowered at her husband. 'It's because of you I'm in this mess.'

Hurt swept across Jake's face.

Brian took the father-to-be's arm. 'Come on, son. Let's go and find the conductor. He can radio ahead and have an ambulance waiting at the next stop.'

'This can't be happening,' Lexi said, as Jake disappeared from view. 'I can't give birth here.' Tears sprang in her eyes. 'I told him we'd be better staying at home. Why didn't he listen?'

'Everything's going to be fine,' I said. 'The train will be on the move again soon and you'll be at the hospital before you know it.'

'I hope you're right,' Martha said. Her voice almost a whisper, she seemed to instinctively put a hand on her tummy.

My heart went out to her and realising she needed to be kept busy for her own sake as much as Lexi's, I reached for my tote bag and pulled out my knitting. 'How are you at this?' I asked.

Martha stared at the needles, confused. 'I can knit and purl, if that's what you mean?'

'Can you cast off?'

Martha nodded.

I passed everything over. 'Away you go then. We'll need something to wrap the baby in when the time comes.'

Clearly appreciating the distraction, Martha settled herself down, took a deep breath and got to it.

Lexi grimaced as another pain welled in her belly.

CHAPTER 37

*L*exi's groans had grown louder and her face more contorted. She'd managed to walk through a lot of her pain by pacing up and down the aisle. However, as time had gone on her contractions hadn't just become longer, stronger and more frequent, they were stopping her in her tracks.

Lexi's worsening discomfort made me feel powerless, but I knew my feelings were nothing compared to what Jake was going through. As I watched him step forward for the umpteenth time, Lexi flashed him a scowl to yet again tell him his assistance wasn't wanted. Seeing the poor man's desperation, I gave him a reassuring pat on the arm as he retook his seat.

Alex and I each checked the clocks on our phone screens and noting Lexi's contractions now stood at less than five minutes apart, we shared a look of concern.

Alex took a deep breath. 'Looks like we're almost there.'

'We can't be,' Lexi said.

'Shouldn't we wait until we get to the next station?' Jake asked. The poor man was beside himself.

'That would be my preferred option,' Julia said under her breath.

'There isn't time.' Alex put a hand on Lexi's shoulder. 'Everything's gonna be okay. I just need you to trust me.'

Lexi swallowed hard and nodded.

Martha sped up her knitting.

'You too, daddy.' Alex took a deep breath, returning his attention to the mother-to-be. 'Right, let's get you comfortable.'

'Good idea,' Jake said. He frantically scanned the train. 'How? Where? Jesus Christ, this can't be happening.' Grabbing every coat he could see, his hands shook as he spread them out on a row of seats.

Lexi grimaced as pain yet again seared through her belly.

'She can't lie down,' Alex said.

'Why not?' I asked.

'The uterus pushes on major blood vessels,' Alex replied. 'If she's on her back she'll faint.'

Clearly feeling useless, Jake visibly deflated.

'Why don't we go and chase up the conductor?' Brian asked him. 'He can sort us out with some towels.'

At last, Lexi's contraction subsided.

'When you're ready,' Alex said. 'You need to take off your...' He indicated Lexi's nether region.

Julia grimaced. 'Thank God she's wearing a dress.'

I spun round and glared at her. 'If that's your only contribution, I suggest you keep your mouth shut.'

I turned my disapproval on Gideon, who sat there wide-eyed and silent. I shook my head, realising what a lucky escape I'd had. He was utterly useless.

A mix of horror and panic crossed Lexi's face. 'I need to push!'

As she latched on to Alex's hand, he winced at the strength with which Lexi gripped it.

Martha worked even faster.

'Now!' Lexi added.

As Alex nodded for me to get into position, I blew my fringe out of the way and crouched down.

Alex flinched as Lexi squeezed his hand even tighter. Using her other, she grabbed the headrest of the seat next to her. Lexi screwed up her face and she turned red as she held her breath and bore down. Finally, the contraction subsided and she, at last, breathed again.

'You're doing brilliantly,' I said.

'Remember to pant.' Taking short breaths, Alex demonstrated what Lexi needed to do.

Keeping her eyes on him, she followed his lead.

The carriage doors swished open, and Jake, Brian and the conductor appeared.

'I haven't missed it, have I?' Jake asked, rushing forward.

'Don't you dare come near me,' Lexi said, her voice hissing.

Jake stopped still.

'No towels. But we have a first aid kit and a foil blanket.' Holding them out, like Jake, Brian was hesitant to take another step closer.

Awestruck, the conductor had no such problem. 'This is one Christmas Eve I'm not likely to forget.' His face beamed as he looked around the group. 'The wife's not gonna believe it when I tell her.'

'Jake,' Alex said. 'We need you to keep an eye on the time.'

Jake appeared confused.

'So you have a record of when your baby's born.'

As Jake frantically dug into his pocket and pulled out his phone, I thanked God for Alex's foresight. Not something I'd have thought of, it was good to know one of us had a clear head. And now Jake had a role.

'Here comes another one,' Lexi said, grimacing. Again, she pushed with all her might.

With her contractions coming thick and fast, the poor woman worked hard through them all. 'I can't do this,' she eventually said. Growing weaker, her energy levels seemed to border on empty.

'Yes, you can,' Alex said, his voice calm and encouraging. 'You've got this.'

Lexi steeled herself as another contraction took hold of her body.

'Time to cast off, Martha,' I called out. 'I can see the baby's head.' Joy and anticipation threatened to overwhelm me as I looked up at the mum-to-be. 'We're almost there, Lexi.' I watched the baby make a quarter turn. 'Yep. We're definitely almost there.'

Martha worked her knitting needles at double speed.

Jake kept his eyes on the time.

'One big push,' Alex said.

Lexi steeled herself as another contraction began. The poor woman looked exhausted.

'Push, push, push,' Alex said.

Lexi gave everything she had and as I pulled the baby free, tears filled my eyes. 'It's a boy,' I said, as he cried out.

A sob escaped Lexi's mouth.

'What time is it, Daddy?' Alex asked.

'12.01am,' Jake said. He glanced around, his expression filled with pride and relief. 'We have a Christmas Day baby.'

With nothing else to hand, I grabbed Julia's angora scarf and ignoring her protests, used it to quickly dry the tiny bundle of joy, while Brian gathered the coats into a pile.

'We need to cut the cord,' Alex said.

Trying to recall every birthing scene I'd watched on television, I pulled out my scissors. Blanket complete, Martha handed me what was left of the ball of wool and I cut two strands. Tying one around the umbilical nearer to the baby and one towards the placenta, I looked to Jake. 'Daddy.' I held out the scissors for him to take. 'Would you like to do the honours?'

His hands shook as he cut between the two ties.

Alex guided Lexi down so she could lean against Brian's makeshift pillow and once she was settled, I passed her her son.

She unbuttoned her dress so he could lie on her chest, skin to skin.

'You did it,' Jake said, his voice choked. Wiping the tears in his eyes, he looked at Lexi with such awe.

She returned his gaze. 'We did it.' Her voice soft, she smiled as she patted the side of her seat so he could join her.

I felt Alex's arm wrap around my shoulders, and as we both stood in admiration of the new family, I rested my head against his chest.

CHAPTER 38

I smiled as Martha helped Lexi wrap her baby in the blanket that I'd started and she had finished. She ran a finger down the baby's cheek and squeezed the new mum's hand. As she moved out of the way so Jake could retake his position, the train engine suddenly fired up.

'Looks like we're off,' the conductor said.

'At last,' Julia said. 'The quicker I'm out of this train, the better.'

The conductor placed a hand on Jake's arm. 'I'll ring ahead again to double check the ambulance is ready and waiting for you.'

'Thank you,' Jake said. 'That's appreciated.'

'Just so you know, it won't take long. We'll be there in a few minutes.' The conductor hesitated and taking off his Santa hat, handed it to Jake. 'A memento.' He ran a hand through his hair to tidy it. 'Something to give him when he's older.' Taking one last look at the newborn baby, the conductor let out a contented sigh. 'This is definitely one for the record books.' Pulling himself together, he headed off to the next carriage.

As a calmness settled around us, I watched Jake kiss first his child's forehead, and then his wife's. I couldn't just see the love he had for his little family, as it permeated the air; I could feel it. He pushed Lexi's damp fringe to one side, while she reached up and wiped away his tears of joy. Quietly envious of the bond they shared, I wondered if anyone would ever hold that much love in their heart for me.

As if he had read my mind and taken pity, Alex's hand wrapped around mine.

'Thank you,' Lexi said, cradling her baby. 'To all of you.'

Julia bristled. 'No, *thank you*.' She scowled. 'For putting me off having children for life.'

'It's a good blooming job,' Brian said. 'I don't imagine you're cut out for parenthood.'

Forced to agree with him, I doubted Gideon was built for it either. Sat with a glassy stare, that evening's experience had clearly traumatised him. He looked like he'd checked out of reality.

'I don't think any of us will forget tonight in a hurry.' Alex gave me a playful nudge. 'What are the odds we'll be telling our grandchildren about this one day?'

My eyes widened in mock surprise. 'Well that's a bit presumptuous.'

Alex's cheeks reddened. 'I'm not suggesting the two of us will... What I mean is... You know... You telling yours and me telling...'

I grinned.

Alex shook his head. 'You knew exactly what I was saying, didn't you?'

Martha reached into her bag and taking out a pen and piece of scrap of paper, wrote something down. 'Our contact details,' she said to Jake and Lexi. 'So you can keep in touch.' She turned to the rest of us. 'I think we'd all like to know how these three get on, wouldn't we?' She passed the pen and paper to Alex, who wrote on it and handed it to me.

Scribbling down my name and email address, without thinking I tried to give the pen to Gideon and Julia. Julia shook her head and grimaced, while Gideon stared at me as if in a trance. Shrugging, I passed the scrap of paper back to Martha, who, in turn, folded it and gave it to Jake.

'You keep that safe,' she said. 'And remember, we want regular updates.'

Jake duly tucked it into his trouser pocket. 'You can count on them.'

'Have you decided on a name yet?' Brian asked, curious.

Lexi looked to Jake, her eyes full of anticipation.

He discreetly nodded.

'We were thinking, that's if you don't mind, Alex, we might call him after you?'

'Really?' Alex's face broke into a smile and holding his chin high, he puffed his chest out. 'I'd be honoured.'

The train slowed, signalling the end of our evening excitement.

'Looks like this is us,' Jake said. He looked from Alex to me to Martha and Brian and rising to his feet gave each of us a hug. 'I honestly can't thank you all enough. We couldn't have got through this without you.'

Lexi handed him their baby so she could button herself up in readiness of their departure.

'Why don't we help you with your things,' I said.

Giving Lexi her privacy Alex, Martha, Brian and I got to our feet to gather the new parents' belongings.

I wasn't quite ready to say goodbye when the train came to a standstill and the exit doors opened enabling two paramedics wearing Christmas hats to step on board.

The first one smiled at the scene that met him. 'I bet none of you expected this tonight, eh?'

His colleague, jump bag at the ready, immediately checked over Lexi and the baby.

Alex leaned in and I heard him say something about the placenta.

The paramedic checked his watch. 'Any moment now, I'd say.' He smiled at Lexi. 'Time to let these people get on with their Christmases, don't you think?'

Julia scoffed. 'I'm not sure some of us can, after that experience.'

'I think it's been marvellous,' Gideon said, as if waking up from a wonderful dream.

Seeing Gideon's mental state, the second paramedic chuckled. 'Came as a bit of a shock, did it?'

Alex smirked. 'Something like that.'

As the ambulance staff helped Lexi, Jake and their baby from the train, I wondered if I should get off with them. Thanks to Gideon and Julia, it wasn't as if I needed to complete my journey. I considered the long cold night ahead, supposing if I stayed put, I could at least enjoy the relative warmth of the carriage a little longer.

Despite my predicament, as we waved everyone off and retook our seats, I couldn't help but smile. Never mind telling our grandchildren, Alex and I would no doubt be dining out on the night's events for years. I pictured Erin and Joyce when we told them, wondering if they'd even believe us.

I let out a contented sigh. I was about to experience the worst Christmas Day imaginable, with no clue how I was going to get home. Yet neither issue seemed to matter. Thanks to Lexi, Jake and baby Alex, that year would always go down as one of my most favourite Christmases ever.

Gideon suddenly got up from his seat, an action that pulled me out of my reverie.

'Hattie,' he said. He straightened his hair and tugged on the hem of his shirt to tidy himself up. 'I simply have to say your performance tonight was fantastic.'

Knowing I hadn't acted alone, or been the one directing events, I stared at him, confused as to why he was singling me out. 'It was a team effort, Gideon.' My cheeks reddened at the unnecessary attention.

'I know. But I saw a side of you I'll never forget.'

Julia huffed. 'I doubt *any* of us will forget tonight.'

'You handled everything with such calm.'

'Like I said, we all played our part.'

'Not quite all,' Brian said, gesturing to Julia.

My chest tightened as Gideon lowered himself down onto one knee. 'What are you doing?' I asked. A nervous laugh escaped my lips, wondering if we should call the paramedics back to check him over too.

As Julia's eyes darted from Gideon to me and back again, I looked to everyone else. Experiencing the same disbelief as me, everyone stared at him, jaws slackened.

'Gideon, I think you should get up,' I said, my voice shaking.

Ignoring my plea, he put a hand up to his chest. 'Hattie. Would you please do me the honour of becoming my wife?'

While Alex concentrated on his phone, Martha leaned against Brian's shoulder, the two of them having dozed off. Their tiredness obviously the result of the evening's ups and downs, my adrenaline rush had yet to properly wane. I glanced around the carriage, trying to avoid looking at Gideon and Julia. But as their eyes bored into me, their attention was hard to ignore.

Gideon gave me a slow disbelieving headshake. Sat, arms folded, his expression was mocking, as if turning down his marriage proposal was the biggest mistake of my life.

Mouth pinched, Julia's expression couldn't have been any more scathing if she'd tried. Anyone would have thought I was the interloper in our sorry situation, not the other way round. She, too, sat with her arms crossed over her chest and no doubt, like Gideon, relished the prospect of me spending the night on a train station platform.

I silently scoffed. Looking like a couple of bitter and twisted book ends, they didn't spoil a pair. Revelling in their victimhood, they deserved each other.

I considered the events of the last month, for the first time grateful their affair had taken place. Without it, I'd have never fully understood Erin's words of wisdom when she'd said some relationships weren't supposed to last. People came and went at just the right time.

Gideon had never been able to see beyond himself and while I'd thought he'd been there for me after Gran had passed, we hadn't really connected on any deep or meaningful level. I supposed that was Erin's point. We weren't meant to. Gideon was the bridge that led me from my old life with Gran to my new life without. Be it because I was grieving, I felt beholden, or simple naivety, looking back, I'd been a fool to think we were in it for the long haul.

A part of me wondered if I should thank Julia. Without her, I could have ended up in a relationship that left me lonelier than I'd ever have been on my own.

Unable to stand the weight of their stares any longer, I reached for my belongings and rose to my feet.

Alex looked up from his phone. 'Everything all right?' As he manoeuvred himself out of my way, his expression was one of concern.

I smiled. 'I just need to stretch my legs.'

I headed down the aisle and once through to the next carriage, continued to walk as far away from Gideon and Julia as possible. Finally, my pathway came to an end, and I plonked myself down on the train's very last seat. Resigned to a night of pavement pounding, I looked skyward. 'I hope you're in a chatty mood, Gran,' I said. 'Because I'm going to need someone to talk to.'

The train slowed, and the conductor appeared from his cabin. He jumped back in surprise. 'Jesus, Mary and Joseph.' Clutching his chest with one hand, he chuckled as he grabbed a headrest with his other. 'There's been enough shenanigans this evening without adding a heart attack into the mix.'

'Sorry. I didn't mean to startle you.'

'This journey has been one surprise after another,' the conductor said. 'What with snowdrifts, newborns, and now you.' He shook his head. 'Never mind the last thirty years, after tonight alone I think I've earned this retirement.'

I smiled as he went off to carry out his final duties, at the same time steeling myself for what lay ahead. Aware I'd have to phone Erin at some point, I knew the least I could do was wait until daylight.

The train came to a stop and getting up from my seat, I picked up my tote bag and made my way to the exit. The *door open* button went from red to green and as I pressed it and the door swished open, cold air blew in and whipped around me. Disembarking, everywhere was covered in white but I was no longer in any mood for snow angels and footprint patterns.

Resigned, I doubted there'd be anywhere I could get a room and spotting a snow-free bench under the station canopy, I headed straight for it. Shoving my hands into my pockets, I sat down ready to consider my next move.

I heard voices coming from the car park and looking over, I saw Gideon's parents appear.

'Gideon!' Serena called out as her son got off the train. 'Thank goodness.' She raced towards him. 'We've been so worried.'

I rolled my eyes. Like he'd been in any danger.

Gideon kept his face forward as he marched straight past me. Aware I had nowhere to go, he acted like I was invisible. An onlooker would never have guessed we'd been in a relationship; they'd see nothing but two strangers. I pitied Gideon for his stance. Leaving me on the street was obviously my punishment for rebuffing him.

Watching Julia struggle to keep up, I felt sorry for her too.

Julia might not have been my favourite person in the world, but Gideon acted like she wasn't there either.

'You must be Julia?' Serena said, throwing her arms around the woman.

I let out a laugh, realising I was one-hundred-per-cent right to think I'd invited myself to the Mayhews'.

Clocking me, Serena's smile froze. She turned to her son. 'Isn't that...'

'When you're ready, Mother.' Taking her arm, Gideon steered her back towards the car park.

'Here you are,' Alex said, joining me on the bench. 'I was beginning to think you'd run off into the night.'

I would have done if I'd had somewhere to go. I shivered as cold penetrated my coat.

Alex took off his scarf and as he wrapped it around me, he paused, his face inches away from mine.

Butterflies fluttered in my tummy as I lost myself in his gaze until reality suddenly took hold, and I quickly diverted my attention. 'Were you ever going to tell me about those two?' I nodded in the direction of the car park.

'I wanted to a number of times. Then when I did finally pluck up the courage...'

I cocked my head. 'Did you? When?'

'In the pub the other night.'

Cringing, I closed my eyes for a second. Having assumed he was about to declare his undying love, I recalled how I'd asked him not to.

Alex stuffed his hands under his armpits. 'Would you have believed me if I had said something?'

I thought back to when Erin first suggested Gideon was up to no good. Calling the very idea preposterous, I'd insisted a man like him could never be unfaithful. I chuckled at my own stupidity. 'Probably not. Although your sketch would have given you a compelling argument.'

'I warned him to come clean the evening you introduced us. Although to be honest, I wasn't surprised when he didn't.'

Recalling Gideon's self-serving arrogance, I wasn't surprised either. 'You must think I'm a real idiot.'

Alex looked at me direct. 'Not at all.' He rose to his feet. 'Right, enough of this. Come on. Mum'll be waiting for us.'

I looked at Alex, confused.

'Well we can't stay here. You're one step away from your teeth chattering and my feet are already numb.' He narrowed his eyes. 'You didn't think I'd just leave you, did you? Then again, with the madness of my lot, you might wish I had.' He smiled. 'When it comes to Christmas, the more relaxed the better. Steel yourself, we don't do formal.'

Images of Christmases past with Gran flooded my mind. Having never thought I'd experience anything like them again, tears pricked my eyes.

'Hey,' Alex said, pulling me onto my feet. 'We're not that bad. Besides, you can't talk. I've seen your Christmas tree, remember.'

I didn't know if the evening's events had caught up with me or whether it was down to the relief of having a bed for the night, but I suddenly felt overwhelmed. My eyes teared up even more and I found myself unable to speak.

Alex's expression turned earnest. 'Haven't you realised yet?'

I still couldn't find my voice.

'I'm in love with you, Hattie. I have been since the first day I saw you with your navy duffel coat, green tights and blue wellies.'

I let out a laugh.

Alex raised my chin with his finger and forcing me to properly meet his gaze, his eyes searched mine.

As his words echoed around my head, I wanted to tell him I

felt the same; that he was funny and handsome and smart and most importantly kind. And that my Gran would love him as much as I did. Usually when I was in Alex's company, my mouth seemed to run away with itself, but in that moment, when it mattered more than ever, it failed me.

I felt his other hand press against my back. Drawing me close, his expression intensified, and the now familiar fluttering took hold in my chest. Having been desperate for this moment, my heart quickened in nervous anticipation as, tentative, Alex's soft warm lips brushed against mine. Wanting more, I instinctively wrapped my arms around him and our kiss fell into a passionate rhythm that I didn't want to end.

'Alex!' a female voice called out.

We both froze.

'Put that poor girl down!'

Caught in the act, Alex and I giggled. 'Merry Christmas,' I said.

Continuing to smile, Alex planted a kiss on my forehead. 'I hope you're ready for this.' He raised an eyebrow. 'And don't say I didn't warn you.'

Alex took my hand ready to introduce me to his mum, but I tugged on his arm stopping him from moving. 'Alex, I need to say something first.'

He turned to look at me, his eyes questioning.

I smiled. 'I love you too.'

THE END

ALSO BY SUZIE TULLETT

Holly's Christmas Countdown

A Not So Quiet Christmas

Love on the Run

Tessa Cavendish is Getting Married

Six Steps To Happiness

The French Escape

The Trouble With Words

Little White Lies and Butterflies

ACKNOWLEDGEMENTS

I'd like to thank everyone at Bloodhound Books. You're a great team to work with. Your hard work, dedication and the support you give to your authors is much appreciated. I'd especially like to thank Betsy, Fred, Clare, Tara, Shirley, and Hannah. 'Tis the Season wouldn't be the book it is without you.

A special mention goes to Marion Costin-Ford, midwife extraordinaire. Your knowledge and experience helped me bring baby Alex's arrival to life in a way I couldn't have managed on my own. You'd have thought writing a birthing scene would be easy for a mum of two like me. But as I sat down to do just that, it was clear I'd paid more attention to my suffering than the events going on around me.

Finally, I couldn't finish without saying a big thank you to every single one of my readers. Without you I wouldn't be doing the job I love. I hope my stories continue to make you laugh and, at times, cry. And that they take you to the same happy place they take me as I write them.

Happy reading, everyone!

Suzie x

A NOTE FROM THE PUBLISHER

Thank you for reading this book. If you enjoyed it please do consider leaving a review on Amazon to help others find it too.

We hate typos. All of our books have been rigorously edited and proofread, but sometimes mistakes do slip through. If you have spotted a typo, please do let us know and we can get it amended within hours.

info@bloodhoundbooks.com

www.ingramcontent.com/pod-product-compliance
Lightning Source LLC
Chambersburg PA
CBHW050613190726
48283CB00007B/2400